Dante Gabriel Rossetti

Ballads and Sonnets

Dante Gabriel Rossetti

Ballads and Sonnets

ISBN/EAN: 9783744786898

Printed in Europe, USA, Canada, Australia, Japan

Cover: Foto ©Andreas Hilbeck / pixelio.de

More available books at **www.hansebooks.com**

Ballads and Sonnets.

BY

DANTE GABRIEL ROSSETTI.

QUI LEGIT REGIT

BOSTON:
ROBERTS BROTHERS.
1882.

TO

THEODORE WATTS,

THE FRIEND WHOM MY VERSE WON FOR ME,

These Few More Pages

ARE AFFECTIONATELY INSCRIBED.

CONTENTS.

———◆———

BALLADS.

THE HOUSE OF LIFE.

A SONNET-SEQUENCE.[1]

[1] In this table, the sonnets marked * are those which appeared in the author's former volume.

PART II. CHANGE AND FATE.

LYRICS, &c.

SONNETS.

xvi   *CONTENTS.*

ROSE MARY.

ROSE WARS

ROSE MARY.

Of her two fights with the Beryl-stone :
Lost the first, but the second won.

PART I.

" MARY mine that art Mary's Rose,
Come in to me from the garden-close.
The sun sinks fast with the rising dew,
And we marked not how the faint moon grew ;
But the hidden stars are calling you.

" Tall Rose Mary, come to my side,
And read the stars if you 'd be a bride.
In hours whose need was not your own,
While you were a young maid yet ungrown,
You 've read the stars in the Beryl-stone.

" Daughter, once more I bid you read ;
But now let it be for your own need :
Because to-morrow, at break of day,
To Holy Cross he rides on his way,
Your knight Sir James of Heronhaye.

" Ere he wed you, flower of mine,
For a heavy shrift he seeks the shrine.
Now hark to my words and do not fear ;
Ill news next I have for your ear ;
But be you strong, and our help is here.

" On his road, as the rumor 's rife,
An ambush waits to take his life.
He needs will go, and will go alone ;
Where the peril lurks may not be known ;
But in this glass all things are shown."

Pale Rose Mary sank to the floor : —
" The night will come if the day is o'er ! "
" Nay, heaven takes counsel, star with star,
And help shall reach your heart from afar :
A bride you 'll be, as a maid you are."

The lady unbound her jewelled zone
And drew from her robe the Beryl-stone.
Shaped it was to a shadowy sphere, —
World of our world, the sun's compeer,
That bears and buries the toiling year.

With shuddering light 't was stirred and strewn
Like the cloud-nest of the wading moon :
Freaked it was as the bubble's ball,
Rainbow-hued through a misty pall
Like the middle light of the waterfall.

Shadows dwelt in its teeming girth
Of the known and unknown things of earth ;
The cloud above and the wave around, —
The central fire at the sphere's heart bound,
Like doomsday prisoned underground.

A thousand years it lay in the sea
With a treasure wrecked from Thessaly ;
Deep it lay 'mid the coiled sea-wrack,
But the ocean-spirits found the track :
A soul was lost to win it back.

The lady upheld the wondrous thing : —
" Ill fare " (she said) " with a fiend's-fairing :
But Moslem blood poured forth like wine
Can hallow Hell, 'neath the Sacred Sign ;
And my lord brought this from Palestine.

"Spirits who fear the Blessed Rood
Drove forth the accursed multitude
That heathen worship housed herein, —
Never again such home to win,
Save only by a Christian's sin.

"All last night at an altar fair
I burnt strange fires and strove with prayer;
Till the flame paled to the red sunrise,
All rites I then did solemnize;
And the spell lacks nothing but your eyes."

Low spake maiden Rose Mary : —
"O mother mine, if I should not see !"
"Nay, daughter, cover your face no more,
But bend love's heart to the hidden lore,
And you shall see now as heretofore."

Paler yet were the pale cheeks grown
As the gray eyes sought the Beryl-stone :
Then over her mother's lap leaned she,
And stretched her thrilled throat passionately,
And sighed from her soul, and said, "I see."

Even as she spoke, they two were 'ware
Of music-notes that fell through the air ;
A chiming shower of strange device,
Drop echoing drop, once twice and thrice,
As rain may fall in Paradise.

An instant come, in an instant gone,
No time there was to think thereon.
The mother held the sphere on her knee : —
" Lean this way and speak low to me,
And take no note but of what you see."

" I see a man with a besom gray
That sweeps the flying dust away."
" Ay, that comes first in the mystic sphere ;
But now that the way is swept and clear,
Heed well what next you look on there."

" Stretched aloft and adown I see
Two roads that part in waste-country :
The glen lies deep and the ridge stands tall ;
What 's great below is above seen small,
And the hill-side is the valley-wall."

" Stream-bank, daughter, or moor and moss,
Both roads will take to Holy Cross.
The hills are a weary waste to wage ;
But what of the valley-road's presage ?
That way must tend his pilgrimage."

" As 't were the turning leaves of a book,
The road runs past me as I look ;
Or it is even as though mine eye
Should watch calm waters filled with sky
While lights and clouds and wings went by."

" In every covert seek a spear ;
They 'll scarce lie close till he draws near."
" 'The stream has spread to a river now ;
The stiff blue sedge is deep in the slough,
But the banks are bare of shrub or bough."

" Is there any roof that near at hand
Might shelter yield to a hidden band ? "
" On the further bank I see but one,
And a herdsman now in the sinking sun
Unyokes his team at the threshold-stone."

" Keep heedful watch by the water's edge, —
Some boat might lurk 'neath the shadowed sedge."
" One slid but now 'twixt the winding shores,
But a peasant woman bent to the oars
And only a young child steered its course.

" Mother, something flashed to my sight ! —
Nay, it is but the lapwing's flight. —
What glints there like a lance that flees ? —
Nay, the flags are stirred in the breeze,
And the water 's bright through the dart-rushes.

" Ah ! vainly I search from side to side : —
Woe 's me ! and where do the foemen hide ?
Woe 's me ! and perchance I pass them by,
And under the new dawn's blood-red sky
Even where I gaze the dead shall lie."

Said the mother : " For dear love's sake,
Speak more low, lest the spell should break."
Said the daughter : " By love's control,
My eyes, my words, are strained to the goal ;
But oh ! the voice that cries in my soul ! "

" Hush, sweet, hush ! be calm and behold."
" I see two floodgates broken and old :
The grasses wave o'er the ruined weir,
But the bridge still leads to the breakwater ;
And — mother, mother, O mother dear ! "

The damsel clung to her mother's knee,
And dared not let the shriek go free ;
Low she crouched by the lady's chair,
And shrank blindfold in her fallen hair,
And whispering said, " The spears are there ! "

The lady stooped aghast from her place,
And cleared the locks from her daughter's face.
" More 's to see, and she swoons, alas !
Look, look again, ere the moment pass !
One shadow comes but once to the glass.

" See you there what you saw but now ? "
" I see eight men 'neath the willow-bough.
All over the weir a wild growth 's spread :
Ah me ! it will hide a living head
As well as the water hides the dead.

"They lie by the broken water-gate
As men who have a while to wait.
The chief's high lance has a blazoned scroll, —
He seems some lord of tithe and toll
With seven squires to his bannerole.

"The little pennon quakes in the air,
I cannot trace the blazon there : —
Ah ! now I can see the field of blue,
The spurs and the merlins two and two ; —
It is the Warden of Holycleugh ! "

"God be thanked for the thing we know !
You have named your good knight's mortal foe.
Last Shrovetide in the tourney-game
He sought his life by treasonous shame ;
And this way now doth he seek the same.

"So, fair lord, such a thing you are !
But we too watch till the morning star.
Well, June is kind and the moon is clear :
Saint Judas send you a merry cheer
For the night you lie at Warisweir !

" Now, sweet daughter, but one more sight,
And you may lie soft and sleep to-night.
We know in the vale what perils be :
Now look once more in the glass, and see
If over the hills the road lies free."

Rose Mary pressed to her mother's cheek,
And almost smiled but did not speak ;
Then turned again to the saving spell,
With eyes to search and with lips to tell
The heart of things invisible.

"Again the shape with the besom gray .
Comes back to sweep the clouds away.
Again I stand where the roads divide ;
But now all 's near on the steep hillside,
And a thread far down is the rivertide."

" Ay, child, your road is o'er moor and moss,
Past Holycleugh to Holy Cross.
Our hunters lurk in the valley's wake,
As they knew which way the chase would take :
Yet search the hills for your true love's sake."

" Swift and swifter the waste runs by,
And nought I see but the heath and the sky ;
No brake is there that could hide a spear,
And the gaps to a horseman's sight lie clear ;
Still past it goes, and there 's nought to fear."

" Fear no trap that you cannot see, —
They 'd not lurk yet too warily.
Below by the weir they lie in sight,
And take no heed how they pass the night
Till close they crouch with the morning light."

" The road shifts ever and brings in view
Now first the heights of Holycleugh :
Dark they stand o'er the vale below,
And hide that heaven which yet shall show
The thing their master's heart doth know.

" Where the road looks to the castle steep,
There are seven hill-clefts wide and deep :
Six mine eyes can search as they list,
But the seventh hollow is brimmed with mist ;
If aught were there, it might not be wist."

" Small hope, my girl, for a helm to hide
In mists that cling to a wild moorside :
Soon they melt with the wind and sun,
And scarce would wait such deeds to be done :
God send their snares be the worst to shun."

" Still the road winds ever anew
As it hastens on towards Holycleugh ;
And ever the great walls loom more near,
Till the castle-shadow, steep and sheer,
Drifts like a cloud, and the sky is clear."

" Enough, my daughter," the mother said,
And took to her breast the bending head ;
" Rest, poor head, with my heart below,
While love still lulls you as long ago :
For all is learnt that we need to know.

" Long the miles and many the hours
From the castle-height to the abbey-towers ;
But here the journey has no more dread ;
Too thick with life is the whole road spread
For murder's trembling foot to tread."

She gazed on the Beryl-stone full fain
Ere she wrapped it close in her robe again :
The flickering shades were dusk and dun,
And the lights throbbed faint in unison,
Like a high heart when a race is run.

As the globe slid to its silken gloom,
Once more a music rained through the room ;
Low it splashed like a sweet star-spray,
And sobbed like tears at the heart of May,
And died as laughter dies away.

The lady held her breath for a space,
And then she looked in her daughter's face :
But wan Rose Mary had never heard ;
Deep asleep like a sheltered bird
She lay with the long spell minister'd.

"Ah ! and yet I must leave you, dear,
For what you have seen your knight must hear.
Within four days, by the help of God,
He comes back safe to his heart's abode :
Be sure he shall shun the valley-road."

Rose Mary sank with a broken moan,
And lay in the chair and slept alone,
Weary, lifeless, heavy as lead :
Long it was ere she raised her head
And rose up all discomforted.

She searched her brain for a vanished thing,
And clasped her brows, remembering ;
Then knelt and lifted her eyes in awe,
And sighed with a long sigh sweet to draw : —
" Thank God, thank God, thank God I saw ! "

The lady had left her as she lay,
To seek the Knight of Heronhaye.
But first she clomb by a secret stair,
And knelt at a carven altar fair,
And laid the precious Beryl there.

Its girth was graved with a mystic rune
In a tongue long dead 'neath sun and moon :
A priest of the Holy Sepulchre
Read that writing and did not err ;
And her lord had told its sense to her.

She breathed the words in an undertone : —
" *None sees here but the pure alone.*"
" And oh !" she said, " what rose may be
In Mary's bower more pure to see
Than my own sweet maiden Rose Mary?"

BERYL-SONG.

We whose home is the Beryl,
Fire-spirits of dread desire,
Who entered in
By a secret sin,
'Gainst whom all powers that strive with ours are sterile, —
We cry, Woe to thee, mother !
What hast thou taught her, the girl thy daughter,
That she and none other
Should this dark morrow to her deadly sorrow imperil ?
What were her eyes
But the fiend's own spies,
O mother,
And shall We not fee her, our proper prophet and seër ?

Go to her, mother,
Even thou, yea thou and none other,
Thou, from the Beryl:
Her fee must thou take her,
Her fee that We send, and make her,
Even in this hour, her sin's unsheltered avower.
Whose steed did neigh,
Riderless, bridle-less,
At her gate before it was day?
Lo! where doth hover
The soul of her lover?
She sealed his doom, she, she was the sworn approver, —
Whose eyes were so wondrous wise,
Yet blind, ah! blind to his peril!
For stole not We in
Through a love-linked sin,
'Gainst whom all powers at war with ours are sterile, —
Fire-spirits of dread desire,
We whose home is the Beryl?

PART II.

" PALE Rose Mary, what shall be done
With a rose that Mary weeps upon ? "
" Mother, let it fall from the tree,
And never walk where the strewn leaves be
Till winds have passed and the path is free."

" Sad Rose Mary, what shall be done
With a cankered flower beneath the sun ? "
" Mother, let it wait for the night ;
Be sure its shame shall be out of sight
Ere the moon pale or the east grow light."

" Lost Rose Mary, what shall be done
With a heart that is but a broken one ? "
" Mother, let it lie where it must ;
The blood was drained with the bitter thrust,
And dust is all that sinks in the dust."

" Poor Rose Mary, what shall I do, —
I, your mother, that lovèd you ? "
" O my mother, and is love gone ?
Then seek you another love anon :
Who cares what shame shall lean upon ? "

Low drooped trembling Rose Mary,
Then up as though in a dream stood she.
" Come, my heart, it is time to go ;
This is the hour that has whispered low
When thy pulse quailed in the nights we know.

" Yet O my heart, thy shame has a mate
Who will not leave thee desolate.
Shame for shame, yea and sin for sin :
Yet peace at length may our poor souls win
If love for love be found therein.

" O thou who seek'st our shrift to-day,"
She cried, " O James of Heronhaye —
Thy sin and mine was for love alone ;
And oh ! in the sight of God 't is known
How the heart has since made heavy moan.

" Three days yet ! " she said to her heart ;
" But then he comes, and we will not part.
God, God be thanked that I still could see !
Oh ! he shall come back assuredly,
But where, alas ! must he seek for me ?

" O my heart, what road shall we roam
Till my wedding-music fetch me home ?
For love 's shut from us and bides afar,
And scorn leans over the bitter bar
And knows us now for the thing we are."

Tall she stood with a cheek flushed high
And a gaze to burn the heart-strings by.
'T was the lightning-flash o'er sky and plain
Ere laboring thunders heave the chain
From the floodgates of the drowning rain.

The mother looked on the daughter still
As on a hurt thing that 's yet to kill.
Then wildly at length the pent tears came ;
The love swelled high with the swollen shame,
And their hearts' tempest burst on them.

Closely locked, they clung without speech,
And the mirrored souls shook each to each,
As the cloud-moon and the water-moon
Shake face to face when the dim stars swoon
In stormy bowers of the night's mid-noon.

They swayed together, shuddering sore,
Till the mother's heart could bear no more.
'T was death to feel her own breast shake
Even to the very throb and ache
Of the burdened heart she still must break.

All her sobs ceased suddenly,
And she sat straight up but scarce could see.
"O daughter, where should my speech begin?
Your heart held fast its secret sin :
How think you, child, that I read therein?"

"Ah me ! but I thought not how it came
When your words showed that you knew my shame :
And now that you call me still your own,
I half forget you have ever known.
Did you read my heart in the Beryl-stone?"

The lady answered her mournfully : —
"The Beryl-stone has no voice for me :
But when you charged its power to show
The truth which none but the pure may know,
Did naught speak once of a coming woe?"

Her hand was close to her daughter's heart,
And it felt the life-blood's sudden start :
A quick deep breath did the damsel draw,
Like the struck fawn in the oakenshaw :
"O mother," she cried, "but still I saw !"

"O child, my child, why held you apart
From my great love your hidden heart?
Said I not that all sin must chase
From the spell's sphere the spirits of grace,
And yield their rule to the evil race?

"Ah ! would to God I had clearly told
How strong those powers, accurst of old :
Their heart is the ruined house of lies ;
O girl, they can seal the sinful eyes,
Or show the truth by contraries !"

The daughter sat as cold as a stone,
And spoke no word but gazed alone,
Nor moved, though her mother strove a space
To clasp her round in a close embrace,
Because she dared not see her face.

" Oh ! " at last did the mother cry,
" Be sure, as he loved you, so will I !
Ah ! still and dumb is the bride, I trow ;
But cold and stark as the winter snow
Is the bridegroom's heart, laid dead below !

" Daughter, daughter, remember you
That cloud in the hills by Holycleugh?
'T was a Hell-screen hiding truth away :
There, not i' the vale, the ambush lay,
And thence was the dead borne home to-day."

Deep the flood and heavy the shock
When sea meets sea in the riven rock :
But calm is the pulse that shakes the sea
To the prisoned tide of doom set free
In the breaking heart of Rose Mary.

Once she sprang as the heifer springs
With the wolf's teeth at its red heart-strings :
First 't was fire in her breast and brain,
And then scarce hers but the whole world's pain,
As she gave one shriek and sank again.

In the hair dark-waved the face lay white
As the moon lies in the lap of night ;
And as night through which no moon may dart
Lies on a pool in the woods apart,
So lay the swoon on the weary heart.

The lady felt for the bosom's stir,
And wildly kissed and called on her ;
Then turned away with a quick footfall,
And slid the secret door in the wall,
And clomb the strait stair's interval.

There above in the altar-cell
A little fountain rose and fell :
She set a flask to the water's flow,
And, backward hurrying, sprinkled now
The still cold breast and the pallid brow.

Scarce cheek that warmed or breath on the air,
Yet something told that life was there. .
"Ah ! not with the heart the body dies !"
The lady moaned in a bitter wise ;
Then wrung her hands and hid her eyes.

"Alas ! and how may I meet again
In the same poor eyes the self-same pain?
What help can I seek, such grief to guide?
Ah ! one alone might avail," she cried, —
"The priest who prays at the dead man's side."

The lady arose, and sped down all
The winding stairs to the castle-hall.
Long-known valley and wood and stream,
As the loopholes passed, naught else did seem
Than the torn threads of a broken dream.

The hall was full of the castle-folk ;
The women wept, but the men scarce spoke.
As the lady crossed the rush-strewn floor,
The throng fell backward, murmuring sore,
And pressed outside round the open door.

A stranger shadow hung on the hall
Than the dark pomp of a funeral.
'Mid common sights that were there alway,
As 't were a chance of the passing day,
On the ingle-bench the dead man lay.

A priest who passed by Holycleugh
The tidings brought when the day was new.
He guided them who had fetched the dead ;
And since that hour, unwearièd,
He knelt in prayer at the low bier's head.

Word had gone to his own domain
That in evil wise the knight was slain :
Soon the spears must gather apace
And the hunt be hard on the hunters' trace ;
But all things yet lay still for a space.

As the lady's hurried step drew near,
The kneeling priest looked up to her.
" Father, death is a grievous thing ;
But oh ! the woe has a sharper sting
That craves by me your ministering.

" Alas for the child that should have wed
This noble knight here lying dead !
Dead in hope, with all blessed boon
Of love thus rent from her heart ere noon,
I left her laid in a heavy swoon.

"O haste to the open bower-chamber
That 's topmost as you mount the stair :
Seek her, father, ere yet she wake ;
Your words, not mine, be the first to slake
This poor heart's fire, for Christ's sweet sake !

"God speed !" she said as the priest passed through,
" And I ere long will be with you."
Then low on the hearth her knees sank prone ;
She signed all folk from the threshold-stone,
And gazed in the dead man's face alone.

The fight for life found record yet
In the clenched lips and the teeth hard-set ;
The wrath from the bent brow was not gone,
And stark in the eyes the hate still shone
Of that they last had looked upon.

The blazoned coat was rent on his breast
Where the golden field was goodliest;
But the shivered sword, close-gripped, could tell
That the blood shed round him where he fell
Was not all his in the distant dell.

The lady recked of the corpse no whit,
But saw the soul and spoke to it:
A light there was in her steadfast eyes, —
The fire of mortal tears and sighs
That pity and love immortalize.

" By thy death have I learnt to-day
Thy deed, O James of Heronhaye !
Great wrong thou hast done to me and mine;
And haply God hath wrought for a sign
By our blind deed this doom of thine.

"Thy shrift, alas ! thou wast not to win;
But may death shrive thy soul herein !
Full well do I know thy love should be
Even yet — had life but stayed with thee —
Our honor's strong security."

She stooped, and said with a sob's low stir, —
" Peace be thine, — but what peace for her?"
But ere to the brow her lips were press'd,
She marked, half-hid in the riven vest,
A packet close to the dead man's breast.

'Neath surcoat pierced and broken mail
It lay on the blood-stained bosom pale.
The clot clung round it, dull and dense,
And a faintness seized her mortal sense
As she reached her hand and drew it thence.

'T was steeped in the heart's flood welling high
From the heart it there had rested by :
'T was glued to a broidered fragment gay, —
A shred by spear-thrust rent away
From the heron-wings of Heronhaye.

She gazed on the thing with piteous eyne : —
" Alas, poor child, some pledge of thine !
Ah me ! in this troth the hearts were twain,
And one hath ebbed to this crimson stain,
And when shall the other throb again?"

She opened the packet heedfully ;
The blood was stiff, and it scarce might be.
She found but a folded paper there,
And round it, twined with tenderest care,
A long bright tress of golden hair.

Even as she looked, she saw again
That dark-haired face in its swoon of pain :
It seemed a snake with a golden sheath
Crept near, as a slow flame flickereth,
And stung her daughter's heart to death.

She loosed the tress, but her hand did shake
As though indeed she had touched a snake ;
And next she undid the paper's fold,
But that too trembled in her hold,
And the sense scarce grasped the tale it told.

" My heart's sweet lord," ('t was thus she read,)
" At length our love is garlanded.
" At Holy Cross, within eight days' space,
" I seek my shrift ; and the time and place
" Shall fit thee too for thy soul's good grace.

" From Holycleugh on the seventh day
" My brother rides, and bides away :
" And long or e'er he is back, mine own,
" Afar where the face of fear 's unknown
" We shall be safe with our love alone.

" Ere yet at the shrine my knees I bow,
" I shear one tress for our holy vow.
" As round these words these threads I wind,
" So, eight days hence, shall our loves be twined,
" Says my lord's poor lady, JOCELIND."

She read it twice, with a brain in thrall,
And then its echo told her all.
O'er brows low-fall'n her hands she drew : —
" O God ! " she said, as her hands fell too, —
" The Warden's sister of Holycleugh ! "

She rose upright with a long low moan,
And stared in the dead man's face new-known.
Had it lived indeed ?   She scarce could tell :
'T was a cloud where fiends had come to dwell, —
A mask that hung on the gate of Hell.

She lifted the lock of gleaming hair
And smote the lips and left it there.
" Here's gold that Hell shall take for thy toll !
Full well hath thy treason found its goal,
O thou dead body and damnèd soul ! "

She turned, sore dazed, for a voice was near,
And she knew that some one called to her.
On many a column fair and tall
A high court ran round the castle-hall ;
And thence it was that the priest did call.

" I sought your child where you bade me go,
And in rooms around and rooms below ;
But where, alas ! may the maiden be ?
Fear nought, — we shall find her speedily, —
But come, come hither, and seek with me."

She reached the stair like a lifelorn thing,
But hastened upward murmuring : —
" Yea, Death's is a face that's fell to see ;
But bitterer pang Life hoards for thee,
Thou broken heart of Rose Mary ! "

BERYL-SONG.

We whose throne is the Beryl,
Dire-gifted spirits of fire,
Who for a twin
Leash Sorrow to Sin,
Who on no flower refrain to lour with peril,—
We cry,— O desolate daughter!
Thou and thy mother share newer shame with each other
Than last night's slaughter.
Awake and tremble, for our curses assemble!
What more, that thou know'st not yet,—
That life nor death shall forget?
No help from Heaven,— thy woes heart-riven are sterile!
O, once a maiden,
With yet worse sorrow can any morrow be laden?
It waits for thee,
It looms, it must be,
O lost among women,—
It comes and thou canst not flee.
Amen to the omen,
Says the voice of the Beryl.

Thou sleep'st ?   Awake, —
What dar'st thou yet for his sake,
Who each for other did God's own Future imperil ?
Dost dare to live
'Mid the pangs each hour must give ?
Nay, rather die, —
With him thy lover 'neath Hell's cloud-cover to fly, —
Hopeless, yet not apart,
Cling heart to heart,
And beat through the nether storm-eddying winds together ?
Shall this be so ?
There thou shalt meet him, but may'st thou greet him ?
ah no !
He loves, but thee he hoped never more to see, —
He sighed as he died,
But with never a thought for thee.
Alone !
Alone, for ever alone, —
Whose eyes were such wondrous spies for the fate foreshown !
Lo ! have not We leashed the twin
Of endless Sorrow to Sin, —
Who on no flower refrain to lour with peril, —
Dire-gifted spirits of fire,
We whose throne is the Beryl ?

PART III.

A swoon that breaks is the whelming wave
When help comes late but still can save.
With all blind throes is the instant rife, —
Hurtling clangor and clouds at strife, —
The breath of death, but the kiss of life.

The night lay deep on Rose Mary's heart,
For her swoon was death's kind counterpart :
The dawn broke dim on Rose Mary's soul, —
No hill-crown's heavenly aureole,
But a wild gleam on a shaken shoal.

Her senses gasped in the sudden air,
And she looked around, but none was there.
She felt the slackening frost distil
Through her blood the last ooze dull and chill :
Her lids were dry and her lips were still.

Her tears had flooded her heart again ;
As after a long day's bitter rain,
At dusk when the wet flower-cups shrink,
· The drops run in from the beaded brink,
And all the close-shut petals drink.

Again her sighs on her heart were rolled ;
As the wind that long has swept the wold, —
Whose moan was made with the moaning sea, —
Beats out its breath in the last torn tree,
And sinks at length in lethargy.

She knew she had waded bosom-deep
Along death's bank in the sedge of sleep :
All else was lost to her clouded mind ;
Nor, looking back, could she see defin'd
O'er the dim dumb waste what lay behind.

Slowly fades the sun from the wall
Till day lies dead on the sun-dial :
And now in Rose Mary's lifted eye
'T was shadow alone that made reply
To the set face of the soul's dark sky.

Yet still through her soul there wandered past
Dread phantoms borne on a wailing blast, —
Death and sorrow and sin and shame ;
And, murmured still, to her lips there came
Her mother's and her lover's name.

How to ask, and what thing to know?
She might not stay and she dared not go.
From fires unseen these smoke-clouds curled ;
But where did the hidden curse lie furled?
And how to seek through the weary world?

With toiling breath she rose from the floor
And dragged her steps to an open door :
'T was the secret panel standing wide,
As the lady's hand had let it bide
In hastening back to her daughter's side.

She passed, but reeled with a dizzy brain
And smote the door which closed again.
She stood within by the darkling stair,
But her feet might mount more freely there, —
'T was the open light most blinded her.

Within her mind no wonder grew
At the secret path she never knew:
All ways alike were strange to her now, —
One field bare-ridged from the spirit's plough,
One thicket black with the cypress-bough.

Once she thought that she heard her name;
And she paused, but knew not whence it came.
Down the shadowed stair a faint ray fell
That guided the weary footsteps well
Till it led her up to the altar-cell.

No change there was on Rose Mary's face
As she leaned in the portal's narrow space:
Still she stood by the pillar's stem,
Hand and bosom and garment's hem,
As the soul stands by at the requiem.

The altar-cell was a dome low-lit,
And a veil hung in the midst of it:
At the pole-points of its circling girth
Four symbols stood of the world's first birth, —
Air and water and fire and earth.

To the north, a fountain glittered free ;
To the south, there glowed a red fruit-tree ;
To the east, a lamp flamed high and fair ;
To the west, a crystal casket rare
Held fast a cloud of the fields of air.

The painted walls were a mystic show
Of time's ebb-tide and overflow ;
His hoards long-locked and conquering key,
His service-fires that in heaven be,
And earth-wheels whirled perpetually.

Rose Mary gazed from the open door
As on idle things she cared not for, —
The fleeting shapes of an empty tale ;
Then stepped with a heedless visage pale,
And lifted aside the altar-veil.

The altar stood from its curved recess
In a coiling serpent's life-likeness :
Even such a serpent evermore
Lies deep asleep at the world's dark core
Till the last Voice shake the sea and shore.

From the altar-cloth a book rose spread
And tapers burned at the altar-head ;
And there in the altar-midst alone,
'Twixt wings of a sculptured beast unknown,
Rose Mary saw the Beryl-stone.

Firm it sat 'twixt the hollowed wings,
As an orb sits in the hand of kings :
And lo ! for that Foe whose curse far-flown
Had bound her life with a burning zone,
Rose Mary knew the Beryl-stone.

Dread is the meteor's blazing sphere
When the poles throb to its blind career ;
But not with a light more grim and ghast
Thereby is the future doom forecast,
Than now this sight brought back the past.

The hours and minutes seemed to whirr
In a clanging swarm that deafened her ;
They stung her heart to a writhing flame,
And marshalled past in its glare they came, —
Death and sorrow and sin and shame.

Round the Beryl's sphere she saw them pass
And mock her eyes from the fated glass :
One by one in a fiery train
The dead hours seemed to wax and wane,
And burned till all was known again.

From the drained heart's fount there rose no cry,
There sprang no tears, for the source was dry.
Held in the hand of some heavy law,
Her eyes she might not once withdraw
Nor shrink away from the thing she saw.

Even as she gazed, through all her blood
The flame was quenched in a coming flood :
Out of the depth of the hollow gloom
On her soul's bare sands she felt it boom, —
The measured tide of a sea of doom.

Three steps she took through the altar-gate,
And her neck reared and her arms grew straight :
The sinews clenched like a serpent's throe,
And the face was white in the dark hair's flow,
As her hate beheld what lay below.

Dumb she stood in her malisons, —
A silver statue tressed with bronze :
As the fabled head by Perseus mown,
It seemed in sooth that her gaze alone
Had turned the carven shapes to stone.

O'er the altar-sides on either hand
There hung a dinted helm and brand :
By strength thereof, 'neath the Sacred Sign,
That bitter gift o'er the salt sea-brine
Her father brought from Palestine.

Rose Mary moved with a stern accord
And reached her hand to her father's sword ;
Nor did she stir her gaze one whit
From the thing whereon her brows were knit ;
But gazing still, she spoke to it.

"O ye, three times accurst," she said,
"By whom this stone is tenanted !
Lo ! here ye came by a strong sin's might ;
Yet a sinner's hand that 's weak to smite
Shall send you hence ere the day be night.

"This hour a clear voice bade me know
My hand shall work your overthrow :
Another thing in mine ear it spake, —
With the broken spell my life shall break.
I thank Thee, God, for the dear death's sake !

"And he Thy heavenly minister
Who swayed erewhile this spell-bound sphere, —
My parting soul let him haste to greet,
And none but he be guide for my feet
To where Thy rest is made complete."

Then deep she breathed, with a tender moan : —
"My love, my lord, my only one !
Even as I held the cursed clue,
When thee, through me, these foul ones slew, —
By mine own deed shall they slay me too !

"Even while they speed to Hell, my love,
Two hearts shall meet in Heaven above.
Our shrift thou sought'st, but might'st not bring :
And oh ! for me 't is a blessed thing
To work hereby our ransoming.

"One were our hearts in joy and pain,
And our souls e'en now grow one again.
And O my love, if our souls are three,
O thine and mine shall the third soul be, —
One threefold love eternally."

Her eyes were soft as she spoke apart,
And the lips smiled to the broken heart:
But the glance was dark and the forehead scored
With the bitter frown of hate restored,
As her two hands swung the heavy sword.

Three steps back from her Foe she trod: —
"Love, for thy sake!   In Thy Name, O God!"
In the fair white hands small strength was shown;
Yet the blade flashed high and the edge fell prone,
And she cleft the heart of the Beryl-stone.

What living flesh in the thunder-cloud
Hath sat and felt heaven cry aloud?
Or known how the levin's pulse may beat?
Or wrapped the hour when the whirlwinds meet
About its breast for a winding-sheet?

Who hath crouched at the world's deep heart
While the earthquake rends its loins apart?
Or walked far under the seething main
While overhead the heavens ordain
The tempest-towers of the hurricane?

Who hath seen or what ear hath heard
The secret things unregister'd
Of the place where all is past and done
And tears and laughter sound as one
In Hell's unhallowed unison?

Nay, is it writ how the fiends despair
In earth and water and fire and air?
Even so no mortal tongue may tell
How to the clang of the sword that fell
The echoes shook the altar-cell.

When all was still on the air again
The Beryl-stone lay cleft in twain;
The veil was rent from the riven dome;
And every wind that's winged to roam
Might have the ruined place for home.

The fountain no more glittered free ;
The fruit hung dead on the leafless tree ;
The flame of the lamp had ceased to flare ;
And the crystal casket shattered there
Was emptied now of its cloud of air.

And lo ! on the ground Rose Mary lay,
With a cold brow like the snows ere May,
With a cold breast like the earth till Spring,
With such a smile as the June days bring
When the year grows warm for harvesting.

The death she had won might leave no trace
On the soft sweet form and gentle face :
In a gracious sleep she seemed to lie ;
And over her head her hand on high
Held fast the sword she triumphed by.

'T was then a clear voice said in the room : —
" Behold the end of the heavy doom.
O come, — for thy bitter love's sake blest ;
By a sweet path now thou journeyest,
And I will lead thee to thy rest.

" Me thy sin by Heaven's sore ban
Did chase erewhile from the talisman :
But to my heart, as a conquered home,
In glory of strength thy footsteps come
Who hast thus cast forth my foes therefrom.

" Already thy heart remembereth
No more his name thou sought'st in death :
For under all deeps, all heights above, —
So wide the gulf in the midst thereof, —
Are Hell of Treason and Heaven of Love.

" Thee, true soul, shall thy truth prefer
To blessed Mary's rose-bower :
Warmed and lit is thy place afar
With guerdon-fires of the sweet Love-star
Where hearts of steadfast lovers are : —

" Though naught for the poor corpse lying here
Remain to-day but the cold white bier,
But burial-chaunt and bended knee,
But sighs and tears that heaviest be,
But rent rose-flower and rosemary."

BERYL-SONG.

We, cast forth from the Beryl,
Gyre-circling spirits of fire,
Whose pangs begin
With God's grace to sin,
For whose spent powers the immortal hours are sterile, —
Woe! must We behold this mother
Find grace in her dead child's face, and doubt of none
other
But that perfect pardon, alas! hath assured her guerdon?
Woe! must We behold this daughter,
Made clean from the soil of sin wherewith We had
fraught her,
Shake off a man's blood like water?
Write up her story
On the Gate of Heaven's glory,
Whom there We behold so fair in shining apparel,
And beneath her the ruin
Of our own undoing!
Alas, the Beryl!
We had for a foeman
But one weak woman;

In one day's strife,

Her hope fell dead from her life;

And yet no iron,

Her soul to environ,

Could this manslayer, this false soothsayer imperil!

Lo, where she bows

In the Holy House!

Who now shall dissever her soul from its joy for ever,

While every ditty

Of love and plentiful pity

Fills the White City,

And the floor of Heaven to her feet for ever is given?

Hark, a voice cries "Flee!"

Woe! woe! what shelter have We,

Whose pangs begin

With God's grace to sin,

For whose spent powers the immortal hours are sterile,

Gyre-circling spirits of fire,

We, cast forth from the Beryl?

THE WHITE SHIP.

THE WHITE SHIP.

HENRY I. OF ENGLAND. — 25TH NOV., 1120.

By none but me can the tale be told,
The butcher of Rouen, poor Berold.
  (*Lands are swayed by a King on a throne.*)
'T was a royal train put forth to sea,
Yet the tale can be told by none but me.
  (*The sea hath no King but God alone.*)

King Henry held it as life's whole gain
That after his death his son should reign.

'T was so in my youth I heard men say,
And my old age calls it back to-day.

King Henry of England's realm was he,
And Henry Duke of Normandy.

The times had changed when on either coast
" Clerkly Harry " was all his boast.

Of ruthless strokes full many an one
He had struck to crown himself and his son ;
And his elder brother's eyes were gone.

And when to the chase his court would crowd,
The poor flung ploughshares on his road,
And shrieked : " Our cry is from King to God ! "

But all the chiefs of the English land
Had knelt and kissed the Prince's hand.

And next with his son he sailed to France
To claim the Norman allegiance :

And every baron in Normandy
Had taken the oath of fealty.

'T was sworn and sealed, and the day had come
When the King and the Prince might journey home :

For Christmas cheer is to home hearts dear,
And Christmas now was drawing near.

Stout Fitz-Stephen came to the King, —
A pilot famous in seafaring ;

And he held to the King, in all men's sight,
A mark of gold for his tribute's right.

" Liege Lord ! my father guided the ship
From whose boat your father's foot did slip
When he caught the English soil in his grip,

"And cried : ' By this clasp I claim command
O'er every rood of English land ! '

" He was borne to the realm you rule o'er now
In that ship with the archer carved at her prow :

" And thither I 'll bear, an' it be my due,
Your father's son and his grandson too.

" The famed White Ship is mine in the bay ;
From Harfleur's harbor she sails to-day,

"With masts fair-pennoned as Norman spears
And with fifty well-tried mariners."

Quoth the King : " My ships are chosen each one,
But I 'll not say nay to Stephen's son.

" My son and daughter and fellowship
Shall cross the water in the White Ship."

The King set sail with the eve's south wind,
And soon he left that coast behind.

The Prince and all his, a princely show,
Remained in the good White Ship to go.

With noble knights and with ladies fair,
With courtiers and sailors gathered there,
Three hundred living souls we were :

And I Berold was the meanest hind
In all that train to the Prince assign'd.

The Prince was a lawless shameless youth ;
From his father's loins he sprang without ruth :

Eighteen years till then he had seen,
And the devil's dues in him were eighteen.

And now he cried : " Bring wine from below ;
Let the sailors revel ere yet they row :

" Our speed shall o'ertake my father's flight
Though we sail from the harbor at midnight."

The rowers made good cheer without check ;
The lords and ladies obeyed his beck ;
The night was light, and they danced on the deck.

But at midnight's stroke they cleared the bay,
And the White Ship furrowed the water-way.

The sails were set, and the oars kept tune
To the double flight of the ship and the moon :

Swifter and swifter the White Ship sped
Till she flew as the spirit flies from the dead :

As white as a lily glimmered she
Like a ship's fair ghost upon the sea.

And the Prince cried, " Friends, 't is the hour to sing !
Is a songbird's course so swift on the wing ? "

And under the winter stars' still throng,
From brown throats, white throats, merry and strong,
The knights and the ladies raised a song.

A song, — nay, a shriek that rent the sky,
That leaped o'er the deep ! — the grievous cry
Of three hundred living that now must die.

An instant shriek that sprang to the shock
As the ship's keel felt the sunken rock.

'T is said that afar — a shrill strange sigh —
The King's ships heard it and knew not why.

Pale Fitz-Stephen stood by the helm
'Mid all those folk that the waves must whelm.

A great King's heir for the waves to whelm,
And the helpless pilot pale at the helm !

The ship was eager and sucked athirst,
By the stealthy stab of the sharp reef pierc'd :

And like the moil round a sinking cup,
The waters against her crowded up.

A moment the pilot's senses spin, —
The next he snatched the Prince 'mid the din,
Cut the boat loose, and the youth leaped in.

A few friends leaped with him, standing near.
"Row! the sea 's smooth and the night is clear!"

"What! none to be saved but these and I?"
"Row, row as you 'd live! All here must die!"

Out of the churn of the choking ship,
Which the gulf grapples and the waves strip,
They struck with the strained oars' flash and dip.

'T was then o'er the splitting bulwarks' brim
The Prince's sister screamed to him.

He gazed aloft, still rowing apace,
And through the whirled surf he knew her face.

To the toppling decks clave one and all
As a fly cleaves to a chamber-wall.

I Berold was clinging anear ;
I prayed for myself and quaked with fear,
But I saw his eyes as he looked at her.

He knew her face and he heard her cry,
And he said, " Put back ! she must not die ! "

And back with the current's force they reel
Like a leaf that 's drawn to a water-wheel.

'Neath the ship's travail they scarce might float,
· But he rose and stood in the rocking boat.

Low the poor ship leaned on the tide :
O'er the naked keel as she best might slide,
The sister toiled to the brother's side.

He reached an oar to her from below,
And stiffened his arms to clutch her so.

But now from the ship some spied the boat,
And " Saved ! " was the cry from many a throat.

And down to the boat they leaped and fell :
It turned as a bucket turns in a well,
And nothing was there but the surge and swell.

The Prince that was and the King to come,
There in an instant gone to his doom,

Despite of all England's bended knee
And maugre the Norman fealty !

He was a Prince of lust and pride ;
He showed no grace till the hour he died.

When he should be King, he oft would vow,
He 'd yoke the peasant to his own plough.
O'er him the ships score their furrows now.

God only knows where his soul did wake,
But I saw him die for his sister's sake.

By none but me can the tale be told,
The butcher of Rouen, poor Berold.
    (*Lands are swayed by a King on a throne.*)

'T was a royal train put forth to sea,
Yet the tale can be told by none but me.
 (*The sea hath no King but God alone.*)

And now the end came o'er the waters' womb
Like the last great Day that 's yet to come.

With prayers in vain and curses in vain,
The White Ship sundered on the mid-main :

And what were men and what was a ship
Were toys and splinters in the sea's grip.

I Berold was down in the sea ;
And passing strange though the thing may be,
Of dreams then known I remember me.

Blithe is the shout on Harfleur's strand
When morning lights the sails to land :

And blithe is Honfleur's echoing gloam
When mothers call the children home :

And high do the bells of Rouen beat
When the Body of Christ goes down the street.

These things and the like were heard and shown
In a moment's trance 'neath the sea alone ;

And when I rose, 't was the sea did seem,
And not these things, to be all a dream.

The ship was gone and the crowd was gone,
And the deep shuddered and the moon shone :

And in a strait grasp my arms did span
The mainyard rent from the mast where it ran ;
And on it with me was another man.

Where lands were none 'neath the dim sea-sky,
We told our names, that man and I.

" O I am Godefroy de l'Aigle hight,
And son I am to a belted knight."

" And I am Berold the butcher's son
Who slays the beasts in Rouen town."

Then cried we upon God's name, as we
Did drift on the bitter winter sea.

But lo ! a third man rose o'er the wave,
And we said, "Thank God ! us three may He save !"

He clutched to the yard with panting stare,
And we looked and knew Fitz-Stephen there.

He clung, and "What of the Prince?" quoth he.
"Lost, lost !" we cried.   He cried, "Woe on me !"
And loosed his hold and sank through the sea.

And soul with soul again in that space
We two were together face to face :

And each knew each, as the moments sped,
Less for one living than for one dead :

And every still star overhead
Seemed an eye that knew we were but dead.

And the hours passed ; till the noble's son
Sighed, "God be thy help ! my strength 's foredone !

"O farewell, friend, for I can no more !"
"Christ take thee !" I moaned ; and his life was o'er.

Three hundred souls were all lost but one,
And I drifted over the sea alone.

At last the morning rose on the sea
Like an angel's wing that beat tow'rds me.

Sore numbed I was in my sheepskin coat;
Half dead I hung, and might nothing note,
Till I woke sun-warmed in a fisher-boat.

The sun was high o'er the eastern brim
As I praised God and gave thanks to Him.

That day I told my tale to a priest,
Who charged me, till the shrift were releas'd,
That I should keep it in mine own breast.

And with the priest I thence did fare
To King Henry's court at Winchester.

We spoke with the King's high chamberlain,
And he wept and mourned again and again,
As if his own son had been slain:

5

And round us ever there crowded fast
Great men with faces all aghast :

And who so bold that might tell the thing
Which now they knew to their lord the King?
Much woe I learnt in their communing.

The King had watched with a heart sore stirred
For two whole days, and this was the third :

And still to all his court would he say,
" What keeps my son so long away?"

And they said : " The ports lie far and wide
That skirt the swell of the English tide ;

" And England's cliffs are not more white
Than her women are, and scarce so light
Her skies as their eyes are blue and bright ;

" And in some port that he reached from France
The Prince has lingered for his pleasaùnce."

But once the King asked : " What distant cry
Was that we heard 'twixt the sea and sky? "

And one said : " With suchlike shouts, pardie !
Do the fishers fling their nets at sea."

And one : " Who knows not the shrieking quest
When the sea-mew misses its young from the nest ? "

'Twas thus till now they had soothed his dread,
Albeit they knew not what they said :

But who should speak to-day of the thing
That all knew there except the King?

Then pondering much they found a way,
And met round the King's high seat that day :

And the King sat with a heart sore stirred,
And seldom he spoke and seldom heard.

'T was then through the hall the King was 'ware
Of a little boy with golden hair,

As bright as the golden poppy is
That the beach breeds for the surf to kiss :

Yet pale his cheek as the thorn in Spring,
And his garb black like the raven's wing.

Nothing heard but his foot through the hall,
For now the lords were silent all.

And the King wondered, and said, " Alack !
Who sends me a fair boy dressed in black ?

" Why, sweet heart, do you pace through the hall
As though my court were a funeral ? "

Then lowly knelt the child at the dais,
And looked up weeping in the King's face.

" O wherefore black, O King, ye may say,
For white is the hue of death to-day.

" Your son and all his fellowship
Lie low in the sea with the White Ship."

King Henry fell as a man struck dead ;
And speechless still he stared from his bed
When to him next day my rede I read.

There 's many an hour must needs beguile
A King's high heart that he should smile, —

Full many a lordly hour, full fain
Of his realm's rule and pride of his reign : —

But this King never smiled again.

By none but me can the tale be told,
The butcher of Rouen, poor Berold.
    (*Lands are swayed by a King on a throne.*)
'T was a royal train put forth to sea,
Yet the tale can be told by none but me.
    (*The sea hath no King but God alone.*)

THE KING'S TRAGEDY.

NOTE.

Tradition says that Catherine Douglas, in honor of her heroic act when she barred the door with her arm against the murderers of James the First of Scots, received popularly the name of "Barlass." This name remains to her descendants, the Barlas family, in Scotland, who bear for their crest a broken arm. She married Alexander Lovell of Bolunnie.

A few stanzas from King James's lovely poem, known as *The King's Quhair*, are quoted in the course of this ballad. The writer must express regret for the necessity which has compelled him to shorten the ten-syllabled lines to eight syllables, in order that they might harmonize with the ballad metre.

THE KING'S TRAGEDY.

JAMES I. OF SCOTS. — 20TH FEBRUARY, 1437.

I CATHERINE am a Douglas born,
    A name to all Scots dear ;
And Kate Barlass they 've called me now
    Through many a waning year.

This old arm 's withered now.   'T was once
    Most deft 'mong maidens all
To rein the steed, to wing the shaft,
    To smite the palm-play ball.

In hall adown the close-linked dance
    It has shone most white and fair ;
It has been the rest for a true lord's head,
And many a sweet babe's nursing-bed,
    And the bar to a King's chambère.

Aye, lasses, draw round Kate Barlass,
   And hark with bated breath
How good King James, King Robert's son,
   Was foully done to death.

Through all the days of his gallant youth
   The princely James was pent,
By his friends at first and then by his foes,
   In long imprisonment.

For the elder Prince, the kingdom's heir,
   By treason's murderous brood
Was slain ; and the father quaked for the child
   With the royal mortal blood.

I' the Bass Rock fort, by his father's care,
   Was his childhood's life assured ;
And Henry the subtle Bolingbroke,
Proud England's King, 'neath the southron yoke
   His youth for long years immured.

Yet in all things meet for a kingly man
   Himself did he approve ;
And the nightingale through his prison-wall
   Taught him both lore and love.

For once, when the bird's song drew him close
   To the opened window-pane,
In her bowers beneath a lady stood,
A light of life to his sorrowful mood,
   Like a lily amid the rain.

And for her sake, to the sweet bird's note,
   He framed a sweeter Song,
More sweet than ever a poet's heart
   Gave yet to the English tongue.

She was a lady of royal blood ;
   And when, past sorrow and teen,
He stood where still through his crownless years
   His Scotish realm had been,
At Scone were the happy lovers crowned,
   A heart-wed King and Queen.

But the bird may fall from the bough of youth,
   And song be turned to moan,
And Love's storm-cloud be the shadow of Hate,
When the tempest-waves of a troubled State
   Are beating against a throne.

Yet well they loved ; and the god of Love,
  Whom well the King had sung,
Might find on the earth no truer hearts
  His lowliest swains among.

From the days when first she rode abroad
  With Scotish maids in her train,
I Catherine Douglas won the trust
  Of my mistress sweet Queen Jane.

And oft she sighed, " To be born a King ! "
  And oft along the way
When she saw the homely lovers pass
  She has said, " Alack the day ! "

Years waned, — the loving and toiling years :
  Till England's wrong renewed
Drove James, by outrage cast on his crown,
  To the open field of feud.

'T was when the King and his host were met
  At the leaguer of Roxbro' hold,
The Queen o' the sudden sought his camp
  With a tale of dread to be told.

And she showed him a secret letter writ
  That spoke of treasonous strife,
And how a band of his noblest lords
  Were sworn to take his life.

"And it may be here or it may be there,
  In the camp or the court," she said :
"But for my sake come to your people's arms
  And guard your royal head."

Quoth he, "'T is the fifteenth day of the siege,
  And the castle 's nigh to yield."
"O face your foes on your throne," she cried,
  "And show the power you wield ;
And under your Scotish people's love
  You shall sit as under your shield."

At the fair Queen's side I stood that day
  When he bade them raise the siege,
And back to his Court he sped to know
  How the lords would meet their Liege.

But when he summoned his Parliament,
  The louring brows hung round,

Like clouds that circle the mountain-head
　Ere the first low thunders sound.

For he had tamed the nobles' lust
　And curbed their power and pride,
And reached out an arm to right the poor
　Through Scotland far and wide ;
And many a lordly wrong-doer
　By the headsman's axe had died.

'T was then upspoke Sir Robert Græme,
　The bold o'ermastering man : —
" O King, in the name of your Three Estates
　I set you under their ban !

" For, as your lords made oath to you
　Of service and fealty,
Even in like wise you pledged your oath
　Their faithful sire to be : — ,

" Yet all we here that are nobly sprung
　Have mourned dear kith and kin
Since first for the Scotish Barons' curse
　Did your bloody rule begin."

With that he laid his hands on his King : —
  " Is this not so, my lords ? "
But of all who had sworn to league with him
  Not one spake back to his words.

Quoth the King : — " Thou speak'st but for one Estate,
  Nor doth it avow thy gage.
Let my liege lords hale this traitor hence ! "
  The Græme fired dark with rage : —
" Who works for lesser men than himself,
  He earns but a witless wage ! "

But soon from the dungeon where he lay
  He won by privy plots,
And forth he fled with a price on his head
  To the country of the Wild Scots.

And word there came from Sir Robert Græme
  To the King at Edinbro' : —
" No Liege of mine thou art ; but I see
From this day forth alone in thee
  God's creature, my mortal foe.

"Through thee are my wife and children lost,
  My heritage and lands ;
And when my God shall show me a way,
Thyself my mortal foe will I slay
  With these my proper hands."

Against the coming of Christmastide
  That year the King bade call
I' the Black Friars' Charterhouse of Perth
  A solemn festival.

And we of his household rode with him
  In a close-ranked company ;
But not till the sun had sunk from his throne
  Did we reach the Scotish Sea.

That eve was clenched for a boding storm,
  'Neath a toilsome moon half seen ;
The cloud stooped low and the surf rose high ;
And where there was a line of the sky,
  Wild wings loomed dark between.

And on a rock of the black beach-side,
  By the veiled moon dimly lit,

There was something seemed to heave with life
   As the King drew nigh to it.

And was it only the tossing furze
   Or brake of the waste sea-wold?
Or was it an eagle bent to the blast?
When near we came, we knew it at last
   For a woman tattered and old.

But it seemed as though by a fire within
   Her writhen limbs were wrung;
And as soon as the King was close to her,
   She stood up gaunt and strong.

'T was then the moon sailed clear of the rack
   On high in her hollow dome;
And still as aloft with hoary crest
   Each clamorous wave rang home,
Like fire in snow the moonlight blazed
   Amid the champing foam.

And the woman held his eyes with her eyes: —
   " O King, thou art come at last;
But thy wraith has haunted the Scotish Sea
   To my sight for four years past.

6

" Four years it is since first I met,
    'Twixt the Duchray and the Dhu,
A shape whose feet clung close in a shroud,
    And that shape for thine I knew.

" A year again, and on Inchkeith Isle
    I saw thee pass in the breeze,
With the cerecloth risen above thy feet
    And wound about thy knees.

" And yet a year, in the Links of Forth,
    As a wanderer without rest,
Thou cam'st with both thine arms i' the shroud
    That clung high up thy breast.

" And in this hour I find thee here,
    And well mine eyes may note
That the winding-sheet hath passed thy breast
    And risen around thy throat.

" And when I meet thee again, O King,
    That of death hast such sore drouth, —
Except thou turn again on this shore, —
The winding-sheet shall have moved once more
    And covered thine eyes and mouth.

" O King, whom poor men bless for their King,
  Of thy fate be not so fain ;
But these my words for God's message take,
And turn thy steed, O King, for her sake
  Who rides beside thy rein ! "

While the woman spoke, the King's horse reared
  As if it would breast the sea,
And the Queen turned pale as she heard on the gale
  The voice die dolorously.

When the woman ceased, the steed was still,
  But the King gazed on her yet,
And in silence save for the wail of the sea
  His eyes and her eyes met.

At last he said : — " God's ways are His own ;
  Man is but shadow and dust.
Last night I prayed by His altar-stone ;
To-night I wend to the Feast of His Son ;
  And in Him I set my trust.

" I have held my people in sacred charge,
  And have not feared the sting

Of proud men's hate, — to His will resign'd
Who has but one same death for a hind
   And one same death for a King.

"And if God in His wisdom have brought close
   The day when I must die,
That day by water or fire or air
My feet shall fall in the destined snare
   Wherever my road may lie..

"What man can say but the Fiend hath set
   Thy sorcery on my path,
My heart with the fear of death to fill,
And turn me against God's very will
   To sink in His burning wrath?"

The woman stood as the train rode past,
   And moved nor limb nor eye;
And when we were shipped, we saw her there
   Still standing against the sky.

As the ship made way, the moon once more
   Sank slow in her rising pall;
And I thought of the shrouded wraith of the King,
   And I said, "The Heavens know all."

And now, ye lasses, must ye hear
    How my name is Kate Barlass : —
But a little thing, when all the tale
    Is told of the weary mass
Of crime and woe which in Scotland's realm
    God's will let come to pass.

'T was in the Charterhouse of Perth
    That the King and all his Court
Were met, the Christmas Feast being done,
    For solace and disport.

'T was a wind-wild eve in February,
    And against the casement-pane
The branches smote like summoning hands
    And muttered the driving rain.

And when the wind swooped over the lift
    And made the whole heaven frown,
It seemed a grip was laid on the walls
    To tug the housetop down.

And the Queen was there, more stately fair
    Than a lily in garden set ;

And the King was loth to stir from her side ;
For as on the day when she was his bride,
   Even so he loved her yet.

And the Earl of Athole, the King's false friend,
   Sat with him at the board ;
And Robert Stuart the chamberlain
   Who had sold his sovereign Lord.

Yet the traitor Christopher Chaumber there
   Would fain have told him all,
And vainly four times that night he strove
   To reach the King through the hall.

But the wine is bright at the goblet's brim
   Though the poison lurk beneath ;
And the apples still are red on the tree
Within whose shade may the adder be
   That shall turn thy life to death.

There was a knight of the King's fast friends
   Whom he called the King of Love ;
And to such bright cheer and courtesy
   That name might best behove.

And the King and Queen both loved him well
   For his gentle knightliness ;
And with him the King, as that eve wore on,
   Was playing at the chess.

And the King said, (for he thought to jest
   And soothe the Queen thereby ;) —
" In a book 't is writ that this same year
   A King shall in Scotland die.

" And I have pondered the matter o'er,
   And this have I found, Sir Hugh, —
There are but two Kings on Scotish ground,
   And those Kings are I and you.

" And I have a wife and a newborn heir,
   And you are yourself alone ;
So stand you stark at my side with me
   To guard our double throne.

" For here sit I and my wife and child,
   As well your heart shall approve,
In full surrender and soothfastness,
   Beneath your Kingdom of Love."

And the Knight laughed, and the Queen too smiled ;
 But I knew her heavy thought,
And I strove to find in the good King's jest
 What cheer might thence be wrought.

And I said, " My Liege, for the Queen's dear love
 Now sing the song that of old
You made, when a captive Prince you lay,
And the nightingale sang sweet on the spray,
 In Windsor's castle-hold."

Then he smiled the smile I knew so well
 When he thought to please the Queen ;
The smile which under all bitter frowns
 Of hate that rose between,
For ever dwelt at the poet's heart
 Like the bird of love unseen.

And he kissed her hand and took his harp,
 And the music sweetly rang ;
And when the song burst forth, it seemed
 'T was the nightingale that sang.

" *Worship, ye lovers, on this May:*
  Of bliss your kalends are begun:
Sing with us, Away, Winter, away!
  Come, Summer, the sweet season and sun!
  Awake for shame, — your heaven is won, —
And amorously your heads lift all:
Thank Love, that you to his grace doth call!"

But when he bent to the Queen, and sang
  The speech whose praise was hers,
It seemed his voice was the voice of the Spring
  And the voice of the bygone years.

" *The fairest and the freshest flower*
That ever I saw before that hour,
The which o' the sudden made to start
The blood of my body to my heart.

  *   *   *   *   *

Ah sweet, are ye a worldly creature
Or heavenly thing in form of nature?"

And the song was long, and richly stored
  With wonder and beauteous things;

And the harp was tuned to every change
   Of minstrel ministerings ;
But when he spoke of the Queen at the last,
   Its strings were his own heart-strings.

" *Unworthy but only of her grace,*
   Upon Love's rock that's easy and sure,
In guerdon of all my love's space
   She took me her humble creäture.
   Thus fell my blissful aventure
In youth of love that from day to day
Flowereth aye new, and further I say.

" *To reckon all the circumstance*
   As it happed when lessen gan my sore,
Of my rancor and woful chance,
   It were too long, — *I have done therefor.*
   And of this flower I say no more
But unto my help her heart hath tended
And even from death her man defended."

" Aye, even from death," to myself I said ;
   For I thought of the day when she
Had borne him the news, at Roxbro' siege,
   Of the fell confederacy.

But Death even then took aim as he sang
   With an arrow deadly bright ;
And the grinning skull lurked grimly aloof,
And the wings were spread far over the roof
   More dark than the winter night.

Yet truly along the amorous song
   Of Love's high pomp and state,
There were words of Fortune's trackless doom
   And the dreadful face of Fate.

And oft have I heard again in dreams
   The voice of dire appeal
In which the King then sang of the pit
   That is under Fortune's wheel.

" And under the wheel beheld I there
   An ugly Pit as deep as hell,
That to behold I quaked for fear :
   And this I heard, that who therein fell
   Came no more up, tidings to tell :
Whereat, astound of the fearful sight,
I wist not what to do for fright."

And oft has my thought called up again
  These words of the changeful song : —
"*Wist thou thy pain and thy travàil*
To come, well might'st thou weep and wail!"
  And our wail, O God ! is long.

But the song's end was all of his love ;
  And well his heart was grac'd
With her smiling lips and her tear-bright eyes
  As his arm went round her waist.

And on the swell of her long fair throat
  Close clung the necklet-chain
As he bent her pearl-tir'd head aside,
And in the warmth of his love and pride
  He kissed her lips full fain.

And her true face was a rosy red,
  The very red of the rose
That, couched on the happy garden-bed,
  In the summer sunlight glows.

And all the wondrous things of love
  That sang so sweet through the song
Were in the look that met in their eyes,
  And the look was deep and long.

"'T'was then a knock came at the outer gate,
   And the usher sought the King.
" The woman you met by the Scotish Sea,
   My Liege, would tell you a thing ;
And she says that her present need for speech
   Will bear no gainsaying."

And the King said : " The hour is late ;
   To-morrow will serve, I ween."
Then he charged the usher strictly, and said :
   " No word of this to the Queen."

But the usher came again to the King.
   " Shall I call her back ? " quoth he :
" For as she went on her way, she cried,
   ' Woe ! Woe ! then the thing must be ! ' "

And the King paused, but he did not speak.
   Then he called for the Voidee-cup :
And as we heard the twelfth hour strike,
There by true lips and false lips alike
   Was the draught of trust drained up.

So with reverence meet to King and Queen,
   To bed went all from the board ;

And the last to leave of the courtly train
Was Robert Stuart the chamberlain
  Who had sold his sovereign lord.

And all the locks of the chamber-door
  Had the traitor riven and brast ;
And that Fate might win sure way from afar,
He had drawn out every bolt and bar
  That made the entrance fast.

And now at midnight he stole his way
  To the moat of the outer wall,
And laid strong hurdles closely across
  Where the traitors' tread should fall.

But we that were the Queen's bower-maids
  Alone were left behind ;
And with heed we drew the curtains close
  Against the winter wind.

And now that all was still through the hall,
  More clearly we heard the rain
That clamored ever against the glass
  And the boughs that beat on the pane.

But the fire was bright in the ingle-nook,
    And through empty space around
The shadows cast on the arras'd wall
'Mid the pictured kings stood sudden and tall
    Like spectres sprung from the ground.

And the bed was dight in a deep alcove ;
    And as he stood by the fire
The king was still in talk with the Queen
    While he doffed his goodly attire.

And the song had brought the image back
    Of many a bygone year ;
And many a loving word they said
With hand in hand and head laid to head ;
    And none of us went anear.

But Love was weeping outside the house,
    A child in the piteous rain ;
And as he watched the arrow of Death,
He wailed for his own shafts close in the sheath
    That never should fly again.

And now beneath the window arose
    A wild voice suddenly :

And the King reared straight, but the Queen fell back
 As for þitter dule to dree ;
And all of us knew the woman's voice
 Who spoke by the Scotish Sea.

" O King," she cried, " in an evil hour
 They drove me from thy gate ;
And yet my voice must rise to thine ears ;
 But alas ! it comes too late !

" Last night at mid-watch, by Aberdour,
 When the moon was dead in the skies,
O King, in a death-light of thine own
 I saw thy shape arise.

" And in full season, as erst I said,
 The doom had gained its growth ;
And the shroud had risen above thy neck
 And covered thine eyes and mouth.

" And no moon woke, but the pale dawn broke,
 And still thy soul stood there ;
And I thought its silence cried to my soul
 As the first rays crowned its hair.

"Since then have I journeyed fast and fain
  In very despite of Fate,
Lest Hope might still be found in God's will :
  But they drove me from thy gate.

"For every man on God's ground, O King,
  His death grows up from his birth
In a shadow-plant perpetually ;
  And thine towers high, a black yew-tree,
  O'er the Charterhouse of Perth !"

That room was built far out from the house ;
  And none but we in the room
Might hear the voice that rose beneath,
  Nor the tread of the coming doom.

For now there came a torchlight-glare,
  And a clang of arms there came ;
And not a soul in that space but thought
  Of the foe Sir Robert Græme.

Yea, from the country of the Wild Scots,
  O'er mountain, valley, and glen,
He had brought with him in murderous league
  Three hundred armèd men.

7

The King knew all in an instant's flash ,
　　And like a King did he stand ;
But there was no armor in all the room,
　　Nor weapon lay to his hand.

And all we women flew to the door
　　And thought to have made it fast ;
But the bolts were gone and the bars were gone
　　And the locks were riven and brast.

And he caught the pale pale Queen in his arms
　　As the iron footsteps fell, —
Then loosed her, standing alone, and said,
　　" Our bliss was our farewell ! "

And 'twixt his lips he murmured a prayer,
　　And he crossed his brow and breast ;
And proudly in royal hardihood
Even so with folded arms he stood, —
　　The prize of the bloody quest.

Then on me leaped the Queen like a deer : —
　　" O Catherine, help ! " she cried.

And low at his feet we clasped his knees
　　Together side by side.
"Oh ! even a King, for his people's sake,
　　From treasonous death must hide !"

"For *her* sake most !" I cried, and I marked
　　The pang that my words could wring.
And the iron tongs from the chimney-nook
　　I snatched and held to the King : —
"Wrench up the plank ! and the vault beneath
　　Shall yield safe harboring."

With brows low-bent, from my eager hand
　　The heavy heft did he take ;
And the plank at his feet he wrenched and tore ;
And as he frowned through the open floor,
　　Again I said, " For her sake !"

Then he cried to the Queen, "God's will be done !"
　　For her hands were clasped in prayer.
And down he sprang to the inner crypt ;
And straight we closed the plank he had ripp'd
　　And toiled to smoothe it fair.

(Alas ! in that vault a gap once was
    Wherethro' the King might have fled :
But three days since close-walled had it been
By his will ; for the ball would roll therein
    When without at the palm he play'd.)

Then the Queen cried, " Catherine, keep the door,
    And I to this will suffice ! "
At her word I rose all dazed to my feet,
    And my heart was fire and ice.

And louder ever the voices grew,
    And the tramp of men in mail ;
Until to my brain it seemed to be
As though I tossed on a ship at sea
    In the teeth of a crashing gale.

Then back I flew to the rest ; and hard
    We strove with sinews knit
To force the table against the door ;
    But we might not compass it.

Then my wild gaze sped far down the hall
    To the place of the hearthstone-sill ;

And the Queen bent ever above the floor,
    For the plank was rising still.

And now the rush was heard on the stair,
    And " God, what help ? " was our cry.
And was I frenzied or was I bold ?
I looked at each empty stanchion-hold,
    And no bar but my arm had I !

Like iron felt my arm, as through
    The staple I made it pass : —
Alack ! it was flesh and bone — no more !
'T was Catherine Douglas sprang to the door,
    But I fell back Kate Barlass.

With that they all thronged into the hall,
    Half dim to my failing ken ;
And the space that was but a void before
    Was a crowd of wrathful men.

Behind the door I had fall'n and lay,
    Yet my sense was wildly aware,
And for all the pain of my shattered arm
    I never fainted there.

Even as I fell, my eyes were cast
  Where the King leaped down to the pit;
And lo! the plank was smooth in its place,
  And the Queen stood far from it.

And under the litters and through the bed
  And within the presses all
The traitors sought for the King, and pierced
  The arras around the wall.

And through the chamber they ramped and stormed
  Like lions loose in the lair,
And scarce could trust to their very eyes, —
  For behold! no King was there.

Then one of them seized the Queen, and cried, —
  "Now tell us, where is thy lord?"
And he held the sharp point over her heart:
She drooped not her eyes nor did she start,
  But she answered never a word.

Then the sword half pierced the true true breast:
  But it was the Græme's own son

Cried, " This is a woman, — we seek a man ! "
    And away from her girdle-zone
He struck the point of the murderous steel ;
    And that foul deed was not done.

And forth flowed all the throng like a sea,
    And 't was empty space once more ;
And my eyes sought out the wounded Queen
    As I lay behind the door.

And I said : " Dear Lady, leave me here,
    For I cannot help you now ;
But fly while you may, and none shall reck
    Of my place here lying low."

And she said, " My Catherine, God help thee ! "
    Then she looked to the distant floor,
And clasping her hands, " O God help *him*,"
    She sobbed, " for we can no more ! "

But God He knows what help may mean,
    If it mean to live or to die ;
And what sore sorrow and mighty moan
On earth it may cost ere yet a throne
    Be filled in His house on high.

And now the ladies fled with the Queen ;
   And thorough the open door
The night-wind wailed round the empty room
   And the rushes shook on the floor.

And the bed drooped low in the dark recess
   Whence the arras was rent away ;
And the firelight still shone over the space
   Where our hidden secret lay.

And the rain had ceased, and the moonbeams lit
   The window high in the wall, —
Bright beams that on the plank that I knew
   Through the painted pane did fall
And gleamed with the splendor of Scotland's crown
   And shield armorial.

But then a great wind swept up the skies,
   And the climbing moon fell back ;
And the royal blazon fled from the floor,
   And nought remained on its track ;
And high in the darkened window-pane
   The shield and the crown were black.

And what I say next I partly saw
  And partly I heard in sooth,
And partly since from the murderers' lips
  The torture wrung the truth.

For now again came the armèd tread,
  And fast through the hall it fell ;
But the throng was less : and ere I saw,
  By the voice without I could tell
That Robert Stuart had come with them
  Who knew that chamber well.

And over the space the Græme strode dark
  With his mantle round him flung ;
And in his eye was a flaming light
  But not a word on his tongue.

And Stuart held a torch to the floor,
  And he found the thing he sought ;
And they slashed the plank away with their swords ;
  And O God ! I fainted not !

And the traitor held his torch in the gap,
  All smoking and smouldering ;

And through the vapor and fire, beneath
 In the dark crypt's narrow ring,
With a shout that pealed to the room's high roof
 They saw their naked King.

Half naked he stood, but stood as one
 Who yet could do and dare :
With the crown, the King was stript away, —
The Knight was reft of his battle-array, —
 But still the Man was there.

From the rout then stepped a villain forth, —
 Sir John Hall was his name ;
With a knife unsheathed he leapt to the vault
 Beneath the torchlight-flame.

Of his person and stature was the King
 A man right manly strong,
And mightily by the shoulder-blades
 His foe to his feet he flung.

Then the traitor's brother, Sir Thomas Hall,
 Sprang down to work his worst ;
And the King caught the second man by the neck
 And flung him above the first.

And he smote and trampled them under him ;
   And a long month thence they bare
All black their throats with the grip of his hands
   When the hangman's hand came there.

And sore he strove to have had their knives,
   But the sharp blades gashed his hands.
Oh James ! so armed, thou hadst battled there
   Till help had come of thy bands ;
And oh ! once more thou hadst held our throne
   And ruled thy Scotish lands !   ·

But while the King o'er his foes still raged
   With a heart that nought could tame,
Another man sprang down to the crypt ;
And with his sword in his hand hard-gripp'd,
   There stood Sir Robert Græme.

(Now shame on the recreant traitor's heart
   Who durst not face his King
Till the body unarmed was wearied out
   With two-fold combating !

Ah ! well might the people sing and say,
　　As oft ye have heard aright : —
" *O Robert Græme, O Robert Græme,*
Who slew our King, God give thee shame !"
　　For he slew him not as a knight.)

And the naked King turned round at bay,
　　But his strength had passed the goal,
And he could but gasp : — " Mine hour is come ;
But oh ! to succor thine own soul's doom,
　　Let a priest now shrive my soul ! "

And the traitor looked on the King's spent strength,
　　And said : — " Have I kept my word ? —
Yea, King, the mortal pledge that I gave ?
No black friar's shrift thy soul shall have,
　　But the shrift of this red sword ! "

With that he smote his King through the breast ;
　　And all they three in that pen
Fell on him and stabbed and stabbed him there
　　Like merciless murderous men.

Yet seemed it now that Sir Robert Græme,
　　Ere the King's last breath was o'er,

Turned sick at heart with the deadly sight
  And would have done no more. '

But a cry came from the troop above : —
  " If him thou do not slay,
The price of his life that thou dost spare
  Thy forfeit life shall pay ! "

O God ! what more did I hear or see,
  Or how should I tell the rest?
But there at length our King lay slain
  With sixteen wounds in his breast.

O God ! and now did a bell boom forth,
  And the murderers turned and fled ; —
Too late, too late, O God, did it sound ! —
And I heard the true men mustering round,
  And the cries and the coming tread.

But ere they came, to the black death-gap
  Somewise did I creep and steal ;
And lo ! or ever I swooned away,
Through the dusk I saw where the white face lay
  In the Pit of Fortune's Wheel.

And now, ye Scotish maids who have heard
   Dread things of the days grown old, —
Even at the last, of true Queen Jane
   May somewhat yet be told,
And how she dealt for her dear lord's sake
   Dire vengeance manifold.

'T was in the Charterhouse of Perth,
   In the fair-lit Death-chapelle,
That the slain King's corpse on bier was laid
   With chaunt and requiem-knell.

And all with royal wealth of balm
   Was the body purified;
And none could trace on the brow and lips
   The death that he had died.

In his robes of state he lay asleep
   With orb and sceptre in hand;
And by the crown he wore on his throne
   Was his kingly forehead spann'd.

And, girls, 't was a sweet sad thing to see
   How the curling golden hair,

As in the day of the poet's youth,
　　From the King's crown clustered there.

And if all had come to pass in the brain
　　That throbbed beneath those curls,
Then Scots had said in the days to come
That this their soil was a different home
　　And a different Scotland, girls !

And the Queen sat by him night and day,
　　And oft she knelt in prayer,
All wan and pale in the widow's veil
　　That shrouded her shining hair.

And I had got good help of my hurt :
　　And only to me some sign
She made ; and save the priests that were there
　　No face would she see but mine.

And the month of March wore on apace ;
　　And now fresh couriers fared
Still from the country of the Wild Scots
　　With news of the traitors snared.

And still as I told her day by day,
  Her pallor changed to sight,
And the frost grew to a furnace-flame
  That burnt her visage white.

And evermore as I brought her word,
  She bent to her dead King James,
And in the cold ear with fire-drawn breath
  She spoke the traitors' names.

But when the name of Sir Robert Græme
  Was the one she had to give,
I ran to hold her up from the floor;
  For the froth was on her lips, and sore
  I feared that she could not live.

And the month of March wore nigh to its end,
  And still was the death-pall spread;
For she would not bury her slaughtered lord
  Till his slayers all were dead.

And now of their dooms dread tidings came,
  And of torments fierce and dire;
And nought she spake,—she had ceased to speak,—
  But her eyes were a soul on fire.

But when I told her the bitter end
 Of the stern and just award,
She leaned o'er the bier, and thrice three times
 She kissed the lips of her lord.

And then she said, — "My King, they are dead!"
 And she knelt on the chapel-floor,
And whispered low with a strange proud smile, —
 "James, James, they suffered more!"

Last she stood up to her queenly height,
 But she shook like an autumn leaf,
As though the fire wherein she burned
Then left her body, and all were turned
 To winter of life-long grief.

And "O James!" she said, — "My James!" she
  said, —
 "Alas for the woful thing,
That a poet true and a friend of man,
In desperate days of bale and ban,
 Should needs be born a King!"

THE HOUSE OF LIFE:

A SONNET–SEQUENCE.

———

PART I.

YOUTH AND CHANGE.

PART II.

CHANGE AND FATE.

(The present full series of *The House of Life* consists of son-nets only. It will be evident that many among those now first added are still the work of earlier years.)

A Sonnet is a moment's monument, —
   Memorial from the Soul's eternity
   To one dead deathless hour. Look that it be,
Whether for lustral rite or dire portent,
Of its own arduous fulness reverent:
   Carve it in ivory or in ebony,
      As Day or Night may rule; and let Time see
Its flowering crest impearled and orient.

A Sonnet is a coin : its face reveals
   The soul, — its converse, to what Power 't is due : —
Whether for tribute to the august appeals
   Of Life, or dower in Love's high retinue,
It serve; or, 'mid the dark wharf's cavernous breath,
In Charon's palm it pay the toll to Death.

PART I.

YOUTH AND CHANGE.

SONNET I.

LOVE ENTHRONED.

I MARKED all kindred Powers the heart finds fair : —
  Truth, with awed lips ; and Hope, with eyes upcast ;
  And Fame, whose loud wings fan the ashen Past
To signal-fires, Oblivion's flight to scare ;
And Youth, with still some single golden hair
  Unto his shoulder clinging, since the last
  Embrace wherein two sweet arms held him fast ;
And Life, still wreathing flowers for Death to wear.

Love's throne was not with these ; but far above
  All passionate wind of welcome and farewell
He sat in breathless bowers they dream not of ; ·
  Though Truth foreknow Love's heart, and Hope fore-
    tell,
  And Fame be for Love's sake desirable,
And Youth be dear, and Life be sweet to Love.

SONNET II.

BRIDAL BIRTH.

As when desire, long darkling, dawns, and first
 The mother looks upon the newborn child,
 Even so my Lady stood at gaze and smiled
When her soul knew at length the Love it nurs'd.
Born with her life, creature of poignant thirst
 And exquisite hunger, at her heart Love lay
 Quickening in darkness, till a voice that day
Cried on him, and the bonds of birth were burst.

Now, shadowed by his wings, our faces yearn
 Together, as his fullgrown feet now range
  The grove, and his warm hands our couch prepare :
Till to his song our bodiless souls in turn
 Be born his children, when Death's nuptial change
  Leaves us for light the halo of his hair.

SONNET III.

LOVE'S TESTAMENT.

O THOU who at Love's hour ecstatically
   Unto my heart dost ever more present,
   Clothed with his fire, thy heart his testament;
Whom I have neared and felt thy breath to be
The inmost incense of his sanctuary;
   Who without speech hast owned him, and, intent
   Upon his will, thy life with mine hast blent,
And murmured, "I am thine, thou 'rt one with me!"

O what from thee the grace, to me the prize,
   And what to Love the glory, — when the whole
   Of the deep stair thou tread'st to the dim shoal
And weary water of the place of sighs,
And there dost work deliverance, as thine eyes
   Draw up my prisoned spirit to thy soul!

LOVESIGHT.

WHEN do I see thee most, beloved one?
    When in the light the spirits of mine eyes
    Before thy face, their altar, solemnize
The worship of that Love through thee made known?
Or when in the dusk hours, (we two alone,)
    Close-kissed and eloquent of still replies
    Thy twilight-hidden glimmering visage lies,
And my soul only sees thy soul its own?

O love, my love! if I no more should see
Thyself, nor on the earth the shadow of thee,
    Nor image of thine eyes in any spring, —
How then should sound upon Life's darkening slope
The ground-whirl of the perished leaves of Hope,
    The wind of Death's imperishable wing?

SONNET V.

HEART'S HOPE.

By what word's power, the key of paths untrod,
   Shall I the difficult deeps of Love explore,
   Till parted waves of Song yield up the shore
Even as that sea which Israel crossed dryshod?
For lo ! in some poor rhythmic period,
   Lady, I fain would tell how evermore
   Thy soul I know not from thy body, nor
Thee from myself, neither our love from God.

Yea, in God's name, and Love's, and thine, would I
   Draw from one loving heart such evidence
As to all hearts all things shall signify ;
   Tender as dawn's first hill-fire, and intense
   As instantaneous penetrating sense,
In Spring's birth-hour, of other Springs gone by.

THE KISS.

WHAT smouldering senses in death's sick delay
 Or seizure of malign vicissitude
 Can rob this body of honor, or denude
This soul of wedding-raiment worn to-day?
For lo ! even now my lady's lips did play
 With these my lips such consonant interlude
 As laurelled Orpheus longed for when he wooed
The half-drawn hungering face with that last lay.

I was a child beneath her touch, — a man
 When breast to breast we clung, even I and she, —
 A spirit when her spirit looked through me, —
A god when all our life-breath met to fan
Our life-blood, till love's emulous ardors ran,
 Fire within fire, desire in deity.

SONNET VII.

SUPREME SURRENDER.

To all the spirits of Love that wander by
    Along his love-sown harvest-field of sleep
    My lady lies apparent; and the deep
Calls to the deep; and no man sees but I.
The bliss so long afar, at length so nigh,
    Rests there attained.   Methinks proud Love must weep
    When Fate's control doth from his harvest reap
The sacred hour for which the years did sigh.

First touched, the hand now warm around my neck
    Taught memory long to mock desire : and lo !
    Across my breast the abandoned hair doth flow,
Where one shorn tress long stirred the longing ache :
And next the heart that trembled for its sake
    Lies the queen-heart in sovereign overthrow.

SONNET VIII.

LOVE'S LOVERS.

SOME ladies love the jewels in Love's zone
   And gold-tipped darts he hath for painless play
   In idle scornful hours he flings away;
And some that listen to his lute's soft tone
Do love to vaunt the silver praise their own;
   Some prize his blindfold sight; and there be they
   Who kissed his wings which brought him yesterday
And thank his wings to-day that he is flown.

My lady only loves the heart of Love:
   Therefore Love's heart, my lady, hath for thee
   His bower of unimagined flower and tree:
There kneels he now, and all-anhungered of
Thine eyes gray-lit in shadowing hair above,
   Seals with thy mouth his immortality.

SONNET IX.

PASSION AND WORSHIP.

ONE flame-winged brought a white-winged harp-player
  Even where my lady and I lay all alone ;
  Saying : " Behold, this minstrel is unknown ;
Bid him depart, for I am minstrel here :
Only my strains are to Love's dear ones dear."
  Then said I : " Through thine hautboy's rapturous tone
  Unto my lady still this harp makes moan,
And still she deems the cadence deep and clear."

Then said my lady : " Thou art Passion of Love,
  And this Love's Worship : both he plights to me.
  Thy mastering music walks the sunlit sea :
But where wan water trembles in the grove
And the wan moon is all the light thereof,
  This harp still makes my name its voluntary."

SONNET X.

THE PORTRAIT.

O LORD of all compassionate control,
   O Love ! let this my lady's picture glow
   Under my hand to praise her name, and show
Even of her inner self the perfect whole :
That he who seeks her beauty's furthest goal,
   Beyond the light that the sweet glances throw
   And refluent wave of the sweet smile, may know
The very sky and sea-line of her soul.

Lo ! it is done. Above the enthroning throat
   The mouth's mould testifies of voice and kiss,
   The shadowed eyes remember and foresee.
Her face is made her shrine. Let all men note
   That in all years (O Love, thy gift is this !)
     They that would look on her must come to me.

SONNET XI.

THE LOVE-LETTER.

WARMED by her hand and shadowed by her hair
  As close she leaned and poured her heart through thee,
  Whereof the articulate throbs accompany
The smooth black stream that makes thy whiteness fair, —
Sweet fluttering sheet, even of her breath aware, —
  Oh let thy silent song disclose to me
  That soul wherewith her lips and eyes agree
Like married music in Love's answering air.

Fain had I watched her when, at some fond thought,
  Her bosom to the writing closelier press'd,
  And her breast's secrets peered into her breast;
When, through eyes raised an instant, her soul sought
My soul, and from the sudden confluence caught
  The words that made her love the loveliest.

SONNET XII.

THE LOVERS' WALK.

SWEET twining hedgeflowers wind-stirred in no wise
   On this June day; and hand that clings in hand : —
   Still glades; and meeting faces scarcely fann'd : —
An osier-odored stream that draws the skies
Deep to its heart; and mirrored eyes in eyes : —
   Fresh hourly wonder o'er the Summer land
   Of light and cloud; and two souls softly spann'd
With one o'erarching heaven of smiles and sighs : —

Even such their path, whose bodies lean unto
   Each other's visible sweetness amorously, —
   Whose passionate hearts lean by Love's high decree
Together on his heart for ever true,
As the cloud-foaming firmamental blue
   Rests on the blue line of a foamless sea.

SONNET XIII.

YOUTH'S ANTIPHONY.

" I LOVE you, sweet : how can you ever learn
    How much I love you?" "You I love even so,
    And so I learn it." "Sweet, you cannot know
How fair you are." "If fair enough to earn
Your love, so much is all my love's concern."
    "My love grows hourly, sweet." "Mine too doth
      grow,
    Yet love seemed full so many hours ago !"
Thus lovers speak, till kisses claim their turn.

Ah ! happy they to whom such words as these
    In youth have served for speech the whole day long,
    Hour after hour, remote from the world's throng,
Work, contest, fame, all life's confederate pleas, —
What while Love breathed in sighs and silences
    Through two blent souls one rapturous undersong.

SONNET XIV.

YOUTH'S SPRING–TRIBUTE.

On this sweet bank your head thrice sweet and dear
    I lay, and spread your hair on either side,
    And see the newborn woodflowers bashful-eyed
Look through the golden tresses here and there.
On these debateable borders of the year
    Spring's foot half falters; scarce she yet may know
    The leafless blackthorn-blossom from the snow;
And through her bowers the wind's way still is clear.

But April's sun strikes down the glades to-day;
    So shut your eyes upturned, and feel my kiss
Creep, as the Spring now thrills through every spray,
    Up your warm throat to your warm lips: for this
    Is even the hour of Love's sworn suitservice,
With whom cold hearts are counted castaway.

SONNET XV.

THE BIRTH–BOND.

HAVE you not noted, in some family
   Where two were born of a first marriage-bed,
   How still they own their gracious bond, though fed
And nursed on the forgotten breast and knee?—
How to their father's children they shall be
   In act and thought of one goodwill; but each
   Shall for the other have, in silence speech,
And in a word complete community?

Even so, when first I saw you, seemed it, love,
   That among souls allied to mine was yet
One nearer kindred than life hinted of.
   O born with me somewhere that men forget,
   And though in years of sight and sound unmet,
Known for my soul's birth-partner well enough!

SONNET XVI.

A DAY OF LOVE.

THOSE envied places which do know her well,
    And are so scornful of this lonely place,
    Even now for once are emptied of her grace :
Nowhere but here she is : and while Love's spell
From his predominant presence doth compel
    All alien hours, an outworn populace,
    The hours of Love fill full the echoing space
With sweet confederate music favorable.

Now many memories make solicitous
    The delicate love-lines of her mouth, till, lit
    With quivering fire, the words take wing from it ;
As here between our kisses we sit thus
    Speaking of things remembered, and so sit
Speechless while things forgotten call to us.

SONNET XVII.

BEAUTY'S PAGEANT.

WHAT dawn-pulse at the heart of heaven, or last
    Incarnate flower of culminating day, —
    What marshalled marvels on the skirts of May,
Or song full-quired, sweet June's encomiast ;
What glory of change by nature's hand amass'd
    Can vie with all those moods of varying grace
    Which o'er one loveliest woman's form and face
Within this hour, within this room, have pass'd ?

Love's very vesture and elect disguise
    Was each fine movement, — wonder new-begot
    Of lily or swan or swan-stemmed galiot ;
Joy to his sight who now the sadlier sighs,
Parted again ; and sorrow yet for eyes
    Unborn, that read these words and saw her not.

SONNET XVIII.

GENIUS IN BEAUTY.

BEAUTY like hers is genius. Not the call
   Of Homer's or of Dante's heart sublime, —
   Not Michael's hand furrowing the zones of time, —
Is more with compassed mysteries musical ;
Nay, not in Spring's or Summer's sweet footfall
   More gathered gifts exuberant Life bequeathes
   Than doth this sovereign face, whose love-spell breathes
Even from its shadowed contour on the wall.

As many men are poets in their youth,
   But for one sweet-strung soul the wires prolong
   Even through all change the indomitable song ;
So in likewise the envenomed years, whose tooth
Rends shallower grace with ruin void of ruth,
   Upon this beauty's power shall wreak no wrong.

SONNET XIX.

SILENT NOON.

YOUR hands lie open in the long fresh grass, —
 The finger-points look through like rosy blooms :
 Your eyes smile peace. The pasture gleams and
  glooms
'Neath billowing skies that scatter and amass.
All round our nest, far as the eye can pass,
 Are golden kingcup-fields with silver edge
 Where the cow-parsley skirts the hawthorn-hedge.
'T is visible silence, still as the hour-glass.

Deep in the sun-searched growths the dragon-fly
Hangs like a blue thread loosened from the sky : —
 So this wing'd hour is dropt to us from above.
Oh ! clasp we to our hearts, for deathless dower,
This close-companioned inarticulate hour
 When twofold silence was the song of love.

SONNET XX.

GRACIOUS MOONLIGHT.

EVEN as the moon grows queenlier in mid-space
  When the sky darkens, and her cloud-rapt car
  Thrills with intenser radiance from afar, —
So lambent, lady, beams thy sovereign grace
When the drear soul desires thee.   Of that face
  What shall be said, — which, like a governing star,
  Gathers and garners from all things that are
Their silent penetrative loveliness?

O'er water-daisies and wild waifs of Spring,
  There where the iris rears its gold-crowned sheaf
  With flowering rush and sceptred arrow-leaf,
So have I marked Queen Dian, in bright ring
Of cloud above and wave below, take wing
  And chase night's gloom, as thou the spirit's grief.

SONNET XXI.

LOVE-SWEETNESS.

SWEET dimness of her loosened hair's downfall
   About thy face ; her sweet hands round thy head
   In gracious fostering union garlanded ;
Her tremulous smiles ; her glances' sweet recall
Of love ; her murmuring sighs memorial ;
   Her mouth's culled sweetness by thy kisses shed
   On cheeks and neck and eyelids, and so led
Back to her mouth which answers there for all : —

What sweeter than these things, except the thing
   In lacking which all these would lose their sweet : —
   The confident heart's still fervor : the swift beat -
And soft subsidence of the spirit's wing,
Then when it feels, in cloud-girt wayfaring,
   The breath of kindred plumes against its feet ?

SONNET XXII.

HEART'S HAVEN.

SOMETIMES she is a child within mine arms,
    Cowering beneath dark wings that love must chase, —
    With still tears showering and averted face,
Inexplicably filled with faint alarms :
And oft from mine own spirit's hurtling harms
    I crave the refuge of her deep embrace, —
    Against all ills the fortified strong place
And sweet reserve of sovereign counter-charms.

And Love, our light at night and shade at noon,
    Lulls us to rest with songs, and turns away
    All shafts of shelterless tumultuous day.
Like the moon's growth, his face gleams through his tune ;
And as soft waters warble to the moon,
    Our answering spirits chime one roundelay.

SONNET XXIII.

LOVE'S BAUBLES.

I STOOD where Love in brimming armfuls bore
    Slight wanton flowers and foolish toys of fruit :
    And round him ladies thronged in warm pursuit,
Fingered and lipped and proffered the strange store.
And from one hand the petal and the core
    Savored of sleep ; and cluster and curled shoot
    Seemed from another hand like shame's salute, —
Gifts that I felt my cheek was blushing for.

At last Love bade my Lady give the same :
    And as I looked, the dew was light thereon ;
    And as I took them, at her touch they shone
With inmost heaven-hue of the heart of flame.
    And then Love said : " Lo ! when the hand is hers,
    Follies of love are love's true ministers."

SONNET XXIV.

PRIDE OF YOUTH.

EVEN as a child, of sorrow that we give
　　The dead, but little in his heart can find,
　　Since without need of thought to his clear mind
Their turn it is to die and his to live : —
Even so the winged New Love smiles to receive
　　Along his eddying plumes the auroral wind,
　　Nor, forward glorying, casts one look behind
Where night-rack shrouds the Old Love fugitive.

There is a change in every hour's recall,
　　And the last cowslip in the fields we see
　　On the same day with the first corn-poppy.
Alas for hourly change !　Alas for all
The loves that from his hand proud Youth lets fall,
　　Even as the beads of a told rosary !

SONNET XXV.

WINGED HOURS.

EACH hour until we meet is as a bird
  That wings from far his gradual way along
  The rustling covert of my soul, — his song
Still loudlier trilled through leaves more deeply stirr'd :
But at the hour of meeting, a clear word
  Is every note he sings, in Love's own tongue ;
  Yet, Love, thou know'st the sweet strain suffers wrong,
Full oft through our contending joys unheard.

What of that hour at last, when for her sake
  No wing may fly to me nor song may flow ;
  When, wandering round my life unleaved, I know
The bloodied feathers scattered in the brake,
  And think how she, far from me, with like eyes
Sees through the untuneful bough the wingless skies ?

MID–RAPTURE.

THOU lovely and beloved, thou my love ;
   Whose kiss seems still the first ; whose summoning eyes,
   Even now, as for our love-world's new sunrise,
Shed very dawn ; whose voice, attuned above
All modulation of the deep-bowered dove,
   Is like a hand laid softly on the soul ;
   Whose hand is like a sweet voice to control
Those worn tired brows it hath the keeping of : —

What word can answer to thy word, — what gaze
   To thine, which now absorbs within its sphere
   My worshipping face, till I am mirrored there
Light-circled in a heaven of deep-drawn rays?
   What clasp, what kiss mine inmost heart can prove,
   O lovely and beloved, O my love?

SONNET XXVII.

HEART'S COMPASS.

SOMETIMES thou seem'st not as thyself alone,
But as the meaning of all things that are ;
A breathless wonder, shadowing forth afar
Some heavenly solstice hushed and halcyon ;
Whose unstirred lips are music's visible tone ;
Whose eyes the sun-gate of the soul unbar,
Being of its furthest fires oracular ; —
The evident heart of all life sown and mown.

Even such Love is ; and is not thy name Love ?
Yea, by thy hand the Love-god rends apart
All gathering clouds of Night's ambiguous art ;
Flings them far down, and sets thine eyes above ;
And simply, as some gage of flower or glove,
Stakes with a smile the world against thy heart.

SONNET XXVIII.

SOUL-LIGHT.

WHAT other woman could be loved like you,
　Or how of you should love possess his fill?
　After the fulness of all rapture, still, —
As at the end of some deep avenue
A tender glamour of day, — there comes to view
　Far in your eyes a yet more hungering thrill, —
　Such fire as Love's soul-winnowing hands distil
Even from his inmost ark of light and dew.

And as the traveller triumphs with the sun,
　Glorying in heat's mid-height, yet startide brings
　Wonder new-born, and still fresh transport springs
From limpid lambent hours of day begun ; —
　Even so, through eyes and voice, your soul doth move
　My soul with changeful light of infinite love.

SONNET XXIX.

THE MOONSTAR.

LADY, I thank thee for thy loveliness,
  .Because my lady is more lovely still.
  Glorying I gaze, and yield with glad goodwill
To thee thy tribute ; by whose sweet-spun dress
Of delicate life Love labors to assess
  My lady's absolute queendom ; saying, " Lo !
  How high this beauty is, which yet doth show
But as that beauty's sovereign votaress."

Lady, I saw thee with her, side by side ;
  And as, when night's fair fires their queen surround,
An emulous star too near the moon will ride, —
  Even so thy rays within her luminous bound
  Were traced no more ; and by the light so drown'd,
Lady, not thou but she was glorified.

SONNET XXX.

LAST FIRE.

LOVE, through your spirit and mine what summer eve
   Now glows with glory of all things possess'd,
   Since this day's sun of rapture filled the west
And the light sweetened as the fire took leave?
Awhile now softlier let your bosom heave,
   As in Love's harbor, even that loving breast,
   All care takes refuge while we sink to rest,
And mutual dreams the bygone bliss retrieve.

Many the days that Winter keeps in store,
   Sunless throughout, or whose brief sun-glimpses
   Scarce shed the heaped snow through the naked trees.
This day at least was Summer's paramour,
Sun-colored to the imperishable core
   With sweet well-being of love and full heart's ease.

SONNET XXXI.

HER GIFTS.

HIGH grace, the dower of queens ; and therewithal
  Some wood-born wonder's sweet simplicity ;
  A glance like water brimming with the sky
Or hyacinth-light where forest-shadows fall ;
Such thrilling pallor of cheek as doth enthral
  The heart ; a mouth whose passionate forms imply
  All music and all silence. held thereby ;
Deep golden locks, her sovereign coronal ;
A round reared neck, meet column of Love's shrine
  To cling to when the heart takes sanctuary ;
  Hands which for ever at Love's bidding be,
And soft-stirred feet still answering to his sign : —
  These are her gifts, as tongue may tell them o'er.
  Breathe low her name, my soul ; for that means more.

SONNET XXXII.

EQUAL TROTH.

Not by one measure mayst thou mete our love ;
   For how should I be loved as I love thee ? —
   I, graceless, joyless, lacking absolutely
All gifts that with thy queenship best behove ; —
Thou, throned in every heart's elect alcove,
   And crowned with garlands culled from every tree,
   Which for no head but thine, by Love's decree,
All beauties and all mysteries interwove.

But here thine eyes and lips yield soft rebuke : —
   " Then only," (say'st thou) " could I love thee less,
   When thou couldst doubt my love's equality."
Peace, sweet !   If not to sum but worth we look, —
   Thy heart's transcendence, not my heart's excess, —
     Then more a thousandfold thou lov'st than I.

SONNET XXXIII.

VENUS VICTRIX.

COULD Juno's self more sovereign presence wear
   Than thou, 'mid other ladies throned in grace? —
   Or Pallas, when thou bend'st with soul-stilled face
O'er poet's page gold-shadowed in thy hair?
Dost thou than Venus seem less heavenly fair
   When o'er the sea of love's tumultuous trance
   Hovers thy smile, and mingles with thy glance
That sweet voice like the last wave murmuring there?

Before such triune loveliness divine
   Awestruck I ask, which goddess here most claims
The prize that, howsoe'er adjudged, is thine?
   Then Love breathes low the sweetest of thy names ;
And Venus Victrix to my heart doth bring
Herself, the Helen of her guerdoning.

SONNET XXXIV.

THE DARK GLASS.

NOT I myself know all my love for thee :
　How should I reach so far, who cannot weigh
　To-morrow's dower by gage of yesterday?
Shall birth and death, and all dark names that be
As doors and windows bared to some loud sea,
　Lash deaf mine ears and blind my face with spray ;
　And shall my sense pierce love, — the last relay
And ultimate outpost of eternity?

Lo ! what am I to Love, the lord of all?
　One murmuring shell he gathers from the sand, —
　One little heart-flame sheltered in his hand.
Yet through thine eyes he grants me clearest call
And veriest touch of powers primordial
　That any hour-girt life may understand.

SONNET XXXV.

THE LAMP'S SHRINE.

SOMETIMES I fain would find in thee some fault,
   That I might love thee still in spite of it :
   Yet how should our Lord Love curtail one whit
Thy perfect praise whom most he would exalt?
Alas ! he can but make my heart's low vault
   Even in men's sight unworthier, being lit
   By thee, who thereby show'st more exquisite
Like fiery chrysoprase in deep basalt.

Yet will I nowise shrink ; but at Love's shrine
   Myself within the beams his brow doth dart
   Will set the flashing jewel of thy heart
In that dull chamber where it deigns to shine :
   For lo ! in honor of thine excellencies
   My heart takes pride to show how poor it is.

SONNET XXXVI.

LIFE–IN–LOVE.

NOT in thy body is thy life at all
    But in this lady's lips and hands and eyes ;
    Through these she yields thee life that vivifies
What else were sorrow's servant and death's thrall.
Look on thyself without her, and recall
    The waste remembrance and forlorn surmise
    That lived but in a dead-drawn breath of sighs
O'er vanished hours and hours eventual.

Even so much life hath the poor tress of hair
    Which, stored apart, is all love hath to show
    For heart-beats and for fire-heats long ago ;
Even so much life endures unknown, even where,
    'Mid change the changeless night environeth,
    Lies all that golden hair undimmed in death.

SONNET XXXVII.

THE LOVE-MOON.

" WHEN that dead face, bowered in the furthest years,
　　Which once was all the life years held for thee,
　　Can now scarce bid the tides of memory
Cast on thy soul a little spray of tears, —
How canst thou gaze into these eyes of hers
　　Whom now thy heart delights in, and not see
　　Within each orb Love's philtred euphrasy
Make them of buried troth remembrancers?"

" Nay, pitiful Love, nay, loving Pity!　Well
　　Thou knowest that in these twain I have confess'd
Two very voices of thy summoning bell.
　　Nay, Master, shall not Death make manifest
In these the culminant changes which approve
The love-moon that must light my soul to Love?"

SONNET XXXVIII.

THE MORROW'S MESSAGE.

"Thou Ghost," I said, "and is thy name To-day? —
    Yesterday's son, with such an abject brow ! —
    And can To-morrow be more pale than thou?"
While yet I spoke, the silence answered : "Yea,
Henceforth our issue is all grieved and gray,
    And each beforehand makes such poor avow
    As of old leaves beneath the budding bough
Or night-drift that the sundawn shreds away."

Then cried I : "Mother of many malisons,
    O Earth, receive me to thy dusty bed ! "
    But therewithal the tremulous silence said :
"Lo ! Love yet bids thy lady greet thee once : —
Yea, twice, — whereby thy life is still the sun's ;
    And thrice, — whereby the shadow of death is dead."

SONNET XXXIX.

SLEEPLESS DREAMS.

GIRT in dark growths, yet glimmering with one star,
  O night desirous as the nights of youth !
  Why should my heart within thy spell, forsooth,
Now beat, as the bride's finger-pulses are
Quickened within the girdling golden bar?
  What wings are these that fan my pillow smooth?
  And why does Sleep, waved back by Joy and Ruth,
Tread softly round and gaze at me from far?

Nay, night deep-leaved ! And would Love feign in thee
  Some shadowy palpitating grove that bears
  Rest for man's eyes and music for his ears?
O lonely night ! art thou not known to me,
A thicket hung with masks of mockery
  And watered with the wasteful warmth of tears?

SONNET XL.

SEVERED SELVES.

Two separate divided silences,
   Which, brought together, would find loving voice ;
   Two glances which together would rejoice
In love, now lost like stars beyond dark trees ;
Two hands apart whose touch alone gives ease ;
   Two bosoms which, heart-shrined with mutual flame,
   Would, meeting in one clasp, be made the same ;
Two souls, the shores wave-mocked of sundering seas : —

Such are we now.   Ah ! may our hope forecast
   Indeed one hour again, when on this stream
   Of darkened love once more the light shall gleam ? —
An hour how slow to come, how quickly past, —
Which blooms and fades, and only leaves at last,
   Faint as shed flowers, the attenuated dream.

SONNET XLI.

THROUGH DEATH TO LOVE.

LIKE labor-laden moonclouds faint to flee
   From winds that sweep the winter-bitten wold, —
   Like multiform circumfluence manifold
Of night's flood-tide, — like terrors that agree
Of hoarse-tongued fire and inarticulate sea, —
   Even such, within some glass dimmed by our breath,
   Our hearts discern wild images of Death,
Shadows and shoals that edge eternity.

Howbeit athwart Death's imminent shade doth soar
   One Power, than flow of stream or flight of dove
   Sweeter to glide around, to brood above.
Tell me, my heart, — what angel-greeted door
Or threshold of wing-winnowed threshing-floor
   Hath guest fire-fledged as thine, whose lord is Love?

SONNET XLII.

HOPE OVERTAKEN.

I DEEMED thy garments, O my Hope, were gray,
  So far I viewed thee.   Now the space between
  Is passed at length ; and garmented in green
Even as in days of yore thou stand'st to-day.
Ah God ! and but for lingering dull dismay,
  On all that road our footsteps erst had been
  Even thus commingled, and our shadows seen
Blent on the hedgerows and the water-way.

O Hope of mine whose eyes are living love,
  No eyes but hers, — O Love and Hope the same ! —
    Lean close to me, for now the sinking sun
That warmed our feet scarce gilds our hair above.
  O hers thy voice and very hers thy name !
    Alas, cling round me, for the day is done !

SONNET XLIII.

LOVE AND HOPE.

BLESS love and hope.   Full many a withered year
  Whirled past us, eddying to its chill doomsday ;
  And clasped together where the blown leaves lay,
We long have knelt and wept full many a tear.
Yet lo ! one hour at last, the Spring's compeer,
  Flutes softly to us from some green byeway :
  Those years, those tears are dead, but only they : —
Bless love and hope, true soul ; for we are here.

Cling heart to heart ; nor of this hour demand
  Whether in very truth, when we are dead,
  Our hearts shall wake to know Love's golden head
Sole sunshine of the imperishable land ;
  Or but discern, through night's unfeatured scope,
  Scorn-fired at length the illusive eyes of Hope.

II

SONNET XLIV.

CLOUD AND WIND.

LOVE, should I fear death most for you or me?
  Yet if you die, can I not follow you,
  Forcing the straits of change?   Alas ! but who
Shall wrest a bond from night's inveteracy,
Ere yet my hazardous soul put forth, to be
  Her warrant against all her haste might rue ? —
  Ah ! in your eyes so reached what dumb adieu,
What unsunned gyres of waste eternity?

And if I die the first, shall death be then
  A lampless watchtower whence I see you weep ? —
  Or (woe is me !) a bed wherein my sleep
Ne'er notes (as death's dear cup at last you drain),
The hour when you too learn that all is vain
  And that Hope sows what Love shall never reap?

SONNET XLV.

SECRET PARTING.

BECAUSE our talk was of the cloud-control
   And moon-track of the journeying face of Fate,
   Her tremulous kisses faltered at love's gate
And her eyes dreamed against a distant goal :
But soon, remembering her how brief the whole
   Of joy, which its own hours annihilate,
   Her set gaze gathered, thirstier than of late,
And as she kissed, her mouth became her soul.

Thence in what ways we wandered, and how strove
   To build with fire-tried vows the piteous home
   Which memory haunts and whither sleep may roam, —
They only know for whom the roof of Love
Is the still-seated secret of the grove,
   Nor spire may rise nor bell be heard therefrom.

SONNET XLVI.

PARTED LOVE.

WHAT shall be said of this embattled day
   And armed occupation of this night
   By all thy foes beleaguered, — now when sight
Nor sound denotes the loved one far away?
Of these thy vanquished hours what shalt thou say, —
   As every sense to which she dealt delight
   Now labors lonely o'er the stark noon-height
To reach the sunset's desolate disarray?

Stand still, fond fettered wretch! while Memory's art
   Parades the Past before thy face, and lures
   Thy spirit to her passionate portraitures:
Till the tempestuous tide-gates flung apart
Flood with wild will the hollows of thy heart,
   And thy heart rends thee, and thy body endures.

SONNET XLVII.

BROKEN MUSIC.

THE mother will not turn, who thinks she hears
    Her nursling's speech first grow articulate ;
    But breathless with averted eyes elate
She sits, with open lips and open ears,
That it may call her twice.   'Mid doubts and fears
    Thus oft my soul has hearkened ; till the song,
    A central moan for days, at length found tongue,
And the sweet music welled and the sweet tears.

But now, whatever while the soul is fain
    To list that wonted murmur, as it were
The speech-bound sea-shell's low importunate strain, —
    No breath of song, thy voice alone is there,
O bitterly beloved ! and all her gain
    Is but the pang of unpermitted prayer.

DEATH–IN–LOVE.

THERE came an image in Life's retinue
    That had Love's wings and bore his gonfalon :
    Fair was the web, and nobly wrought thereon,
O soul-sequestered face, thy form and hue !
Bewildering sounds, such as Spring wakens to,
    Shook in its folds ; and through my heart its power
    Sped trackless as the immemorable hour
When birth's dark portal groaned and all was new.

But a veiled woman followed, and she caught
    The banner round its staff, to furl and cling, —
    Then plucked a feather from the bearer's wing,   .
And held it to his lips that stirred it not,
    And said to me, " Behold, there is no breath :
    I and this Love are one, and I am Death."

SONNETS XLIX., L., LI., LII.

WILLOWWOOD.

I.

I SAT with Love upon a woodside well,
   Leaning across the water, I and he ;
   Nor ever did he speak nor looked at me,
But touched his lute wherein was audible
The certain secret thing he had to tell :
   Only our mirrored eyes met silently
   In the low wave ; and that sound came to be
The passionate voice I knew ; and my tears fell.

And at their fall, his eyes beneath grew hers ;
And with his foot and with his wing-feathers
   He swept the spring that watered my heart's drouth.
Then the dark ripples spread to waving hair,
And as I stooped, her own lips rising there
   Bubbled with brimming kisses at my mouth.

II.

AND now Love sang : but his was such a song,
  So meshed with half-remembrance hard to free,
  As souls disused in death's sterility
May sing when the new birthday tarries long.
And I was made aware of a dumb throng
  That stood aloof, one form by every tree,
  All mournful forms, for each was I or she,
The shades of those our days that had no tongue.

They looked on us, and knew us and were known ;
  While fast together, alive from the abyss,
  Clung the soul-wrung implacable close kiss ;
And pity of self through all made broken moan
Which said, " For once, for once, for once alone ! "
  And still Love sang, and what he sang was this : —

III.

" O ye, all ye that walk in Willowwood,
    That walk with hollow faces burning white ;
What fathom-depth of soul-struck widowhood,
    What long, what longer hours, one lifelong night,
Ere ye again, who so in vain have wooed
    Your last hope lost, who so in vain invite
Your lips to that their unforgotten food,
    Ere ye, ere ye again shall see the light !

Alas ! the bitter banks in Willowwood,
    With tear-spurge wan, with blood-wort burning red :
Alas ! if ever such a pillow could
    Steep deep the soul in sleep till she were dead, —
Better all life forget her than this thing,
That Willowwood should hold her wandering ! "

IV

So sang he : and as meeting rose and rose
   Together cling through the wind's wellaway
   Nor change at once, yet near the end of day
The leaves drop loosened where the heart-stain glows, —
So when the song died did the kiss unclose ;
   And her face fell back drowned, and was as gray
   As its gray eyes ; and if it ever may
Meet mine again I know not if Love knows.

Only I know that I leaned low and drank
A long draught from the water where she sank,
   Her breath and all her tears and all her soul :
And as I leaned, I know I felt Love's face
Pressed on my neck with moan of pity and grace,
   Till both our heads were in his aureole.

SONNET LIII.

WITHOUT HER.

WHAT of her glass without her? The blank gray
   There where the pool is blind of the moon's face.
   Her dress without her? The tossed empty space
Of cloud-rack whence the moon has passed away.
Her paths without her? Day's appointed sway
   Usurped by desolate night. Her pillowed place
   Without her? Tears, ah me! for love's good grace,
And cold forgetfulness of night or day.

What of the heart without her? Nay, poor heart,
   Of thee what word remains ere speech be still?
   A wayfarer by barren ways and chill,
Steep ways and weary, without her thou art,
Where the long cloud, the long wood's counterpart,
   Sheds doubled darkness up the laboring hill.

SONNET LIV.

LOVE'S FATALITY.

SWEET Love, — but oh ! most dread Desire of Love
Life-thwarted.   Linked in gyves I saw them stand,
Love shackled with Vain-longing, hand to hand :
And one was eyed as the blue vault above :
But hope tempestuous like a fire-cloud hove
I' the other's gaze, even as in his whose wand
Vainly all night with spell-wrought power has spann'd
The unyielding caves of some deep treasure-trove.

Also his lips, two writhen flakes of flame,
Made moan : " Alas O Love, thus leashed with me !
Wing-footed thou, wing-shouldered, once born free :
And I, thy cowering self, in chains grown tame, —
Bound to thy body and soul, named with thy name, —
Life's iron heart, even Love's Fatality."

SONNET LV.

STILLBORN LOVE.

THE hour which might have been yet might not be,
   Which man's and woman's heart conceived and bore
   Yet whereof life was barren, — on what shore
Bides it the breaking of Time's weary sea?
Bondchild of all consummate joys set free,
   It somewhere sighs and serves, and mute before
   The house of Love, hears through the echoing door
His hours elect in choral consonancy.

But lo! what wedded souls now hand in hand
Together tread at last the immortal strand
   With eyes where burning memory lights love home?
Lo! how the little outcast hour has turned
And leaped to them and in their faces yearned : —
   " I am your child : O parents, ye have come ! "

SONNETS LVI., LVII., LVIII.

TRUE WOMAN.

I. HERSELF.

To be a sweetness more desired than Spring ;
   A bodily beauty more acceptable
   Than the wild rose-tree's arch that crowns the fell ;
To be an essence more environing
Than wine's drained juice ; a music ravishing
   More than the passionate pulse of Philomel ; —
   To be all this 'neath one soft bosom's swell
That is the flower of life : — how strange a thing !

How strange a thing to be what Man can know
   But as a sacred secret ! Heaven's own screen
Hides her soul's purest depth and loveliest glow ;
   Closely withheld, as all things most unseen, —
   The wave-bowered pearl, — the heart-shaped seal of
      green
That flecks the snowdrop underneath the snow.

II. HER LOVE.

SHE loves him ; for her infinite soul is Love,
  And he her lodestar.   Passion in her is
  A glass facing his fire, where the bright bliss
Is mirrored, and the heat returned.   Yet move
That glass, a stranger's amorous flame to prove,
  And it shall turn, by instant contraries,
  Ice to the moon ; while her pure fire to his
For whom it burns, clings close i' the heart's alcove.

Lo ! they are one.   With wifely breast to breast
  And circling arms, she welcomes all command
  Of love, — her soul to answering ardors fann'd :
Yet as morn springs or twilight sinks to rest,
Ah ! who shall say she deems not loveliest
  The hour of sisterly sweet hand-in-hand ?

III. HER HEAVEN.

IF to grow old in Heaven is to grow young,
   (As the Seer saw and said,) then blest were he
   With youth for evermore, whose heaven should be
True Woman, she whom these weak notes have sung.
Here and hereafter, — choir-strains of her tongue, —
   Sky-spaces of her eyes, — sweet signs that flee
   About her soul's immediate sanctuary, —
Were Paradise all uttermost worlds among.

The sunrise blooms and withers on the hill
   Like any hillflower; and the noblest troth
   Dies here to dust. Yet shall Heaven's promise clothe
Even yet those lovers who have cherished still
   This test for love : — in every kiss sealed fast
   To feel the first kiss and forbode the last.

SONNET LIX.

LOVE'S LAST GIFT.

LOVE to his singer held a glistening leaf,
  And said : " The rose-tree and the apple-tree
  Have fruits to vaunt or flowers to lure the bee ;
And golden shafts are in the feathered sheaf
Of the great harvest-marshal, the year's chief,
  Victorious Summer ; aye, and 'neath warm sea
  Strange secret grasses lurk inviolably
Between the filtering channels of sunk reef.

All are my blooms ; and all sweet blooms of love
  To thee I gave while Spring and Summer sang ;
  But Autumn stops to listen, with some pang
From those worse things the wind is moaning of.
  Only this laurel dreads no winter days :
  Take my last gift ; thy heart hath sung my praise."

PART II

CHANGE AND FATE.

SONNET LX.

TRANSFIGURED LIFE.

As growth of form or momentary glance
    In a child's features will recall to mind
    The father's with the mother's face combin'd, —
Sweet interchange that memories still enhance :
And yet, as childhood's years and youth's advance,
    The gradual mouldings leave one stamp behind,
    Till in the blended likeness now we find
A separate man's or woman's countenance : —

So in the Song, the singer's Joy and Pain,
    Its very parents, evermore expand
To bid the passion's fullgrown birth remain,
    By Art's transfiguring essence subtly spann'd ;
    And from that song-cloud shaped as a man's hand .
There comes the sound as of abundant rain.

SONNET LXI.

THE SONG-THROE.

By thine own tears thy song must tears beget,
   O Singer !   Magic mirror thou hast none
   Except thy manifest heart ; and save thine own
Anguish or ardor, else no amulet.
Cisterned in Pride, verse is the feathery jet
   Of soulless air-flung fountains ; nay, more dry
   Than the Dead Sea for throats that thirst and sigh,
That song o'er which no singer's lids grew wet.

The Song-god — He the Sun-god — is no slave
   Of thine : thy Hunter he, who for thy soul
   Fledges his shaft : to no august control
Of thy skilled hand his quivered store he gave :
   But if thy lips' loud cry leap to his smart,
   The inspir'd recoil shall pierce thy brother's heart.

SONNET LXII.

THE SOUL'S SPHERE.

SOME prisoned moon in steep cloud-fastnesses,—
   Throned queen and thralled ; some dying sun whose
      pyre
   Blazed with momentous memorable fire ;—
Who hath not yearned and fed his heart with these ?
Who, sleepless, hath not anguished to appease
   Tragical shadow's realm of sound and sight
   Conjectured in the lamentable night ? . . . . .
Lo ! the soul's sphere of infinite images !

What sense shall count them ?   Whether it forecast
   The rose-winged hours that flutter in the van
   Of Love's unquestioning unrevealèd span,—
Visions of golden futures : or that last
Wild pageant of the accumulated past
   That clangs and flashes for a drowning man.

SONNET LXIII.

INCLUSIVENESS.

THE changing guests, each in a different mood,
  Sit at the roadside table and arise :
  And every life among them in likewise
Is a soul's board set daily with new food.
What man has bent o'er his son's sleep, to brood
  How that face shall watch his when cold it lies? —
  Or thought, as his own mother kissed his eyes,
Of what her kiss was when his father wooed?

May not this ancient room thou sit'st in dwell
  In separate living souls for joy or pain?
  Nay, all its corners may be painted plain
Where Heaven shows pictures of some life spent well ;
  And may be stamped, a memory all in vain,
Upon the sight of lidless eyes in Hell.

SONNET LXIV.

ARDOR AND MEMORY.

THE cuckoo-throb, the heartbeat of the Spring;
   The rosebud's blush that leaves it as it grows
   Into the full-eyed fair unblushing rose;
The summer clouds that visit every wing
With fires of sunrise and of sunsetting;
   The furtive flickering streams to light re-born
   'Mid airs new-fledged and valorous lusts of morn,
While all the daughters of the daybreak sing: —

These ardor loves, and memory: and when flown
   All joys, and through dark forest-boughs in flight
   The wind swoops onward brandishing the light,
Even yet the rose-tree's verdure left alone
Will flush all ruddy though the rose be gone;
   With ditties and with dirges infinite.

SONNET LXV.

KNOWN IN VAIN.

As two whose love, first foolish, widening scope,
   Knows suddenly, to music high and soft,
   The Holy of holies; who because they scoff'd
Are now amazed with shame, nor dare to cope
With the whole truth aloud, lest heaven should ope;
   Yet, at their meetings, laugh not as they laugh'd
   In speech; nor speak, at length; but sitting oft
Together, within hopeless sight of hope
For hours are silent: — So it happeneth
   When Work and Will awake too late, to gaze
After their life sailed by, and hold their breath.
   Ah ! who shall dare to search through what sad maze
   Thenceforth their incommunicable ways
Follow the desultory feet of Death?

SONNET LXVI.

THE HEART OF THE NIGHT.

From child to youth ; from youth to arduous man ;
  From lethargy to fever of the heart ;
  From faithful life to dream-dowered days apart ;
From trust to doubt ; from doubt to brink of ban ; —
Thus much of change in one swift cycle ran
  Till now.   Alas, the soul ! — how soon must she
  Accept her primal immortality, —
The flesh resume its dust whence it began ?

O Lord of work and peace !   O Lord of life !
  O Lord, the awful Lord of will ! though late,
  Even yet renew this soul with duteous breath :
That when the peace is garnered in from strife,
  The work retrieved, the will regenerate,
  This soul may see thy face, O Lord of death !

SONNET LXVII.

THE LANDMARK.

Was *that* the landmark? What, — the foolish well
  Whose wave, low down, I did not stoop to drink,
  But sat and flung the pebbles from its brink
In sport to send its imaged skies pell-mell,
(And mine own image, had I noted well !) —
  Was that my point of turning? — I had thought
  The stations of my course should rise unsought,
As altar-stone or ensigned citadel.

But lo ! the path is missed, I must go back,
  And thirst to drink when next I reach the spring
Which once I stained, which since may have grown black.
  Yet though no light be left nor bird now sing
  As here I turn, I 'll thank God, hastening,
That the same goal is still on the same track.

A DARK DAY.

THE gloom that breathes upon me with these airs
    Is like the drops which strike the traveller's brow
    Who knows not, darkling, if they bring him now
Fresh storm, or be old rain the covert bears.
Ah ! bodes this hour some harvest of new tares,
    Or hath but memory of the day whose plough
    Sowed hunger once, — the night at length when thou,
O prayer found vain, didst fall from out my prayers ?

How prickly were the growths which yet how smooth,
    Along the hedgerows of this journey shed,
Lie by Time's grace till night and sleep may soothe !
    Even as the thistledown from pathsides dead
Gleaned by a girl in autumns of her youth,
    Which one new year makes soft her marriage-bed.

SONNET LXIX.

AUTUMN IDLENESS.

THIS sunlight shames November where he grieves
   In dead red leaves, and will not let him shun
   The day, though bough with bough be over-run.
But with a blessing every glade receives
High salutation ; while from hillock-eaves
   The deer gaze calling, dappled white and dun,
   As if, being foresters of old, the sun
Had marked them with the shade of forest-leaves.

Here dawn to-day unveiled her magic glass ;
   Here noon now gives the thirst and takes the dew ;
Till eve bring rest when other good things pass.
   And here the lost hours the lost hours renew
While I still lead my shadow o'er the grass,
   Nor know, for longing, that which I should do.

SONNET LXX.

THE HILL SUMMIT.

THIS feast-day of the sun, his altar there
  In the broad west has blazed for vesper-song ;
  And I have loitered in the vale too long
And gaze now a belated worshipper.
Yet may I not forget that I was 'ware,
  So journeying, of his face at intervals
  Transfigured where the fringed horizon falls, —
A fiery bush with coruscating hair.

And now that I have climbed and won this height,
  I must tread downward through the sloping shade
And travel the bewildered tracks till night.
  Yet for this hour I still may here be stayed
  And see the gold air and the silver fade
And the last bird fly into the last light.

SONNETS LXXI., LXXII., LXXIII.

THE CHOICE.

I.

EAT thou and drink ; to-morrow thou shalt die.
 Surely the earth, that 's wise being very old,
 Needs not our help. Then loose me, love, and hold
Thy sultry hair up from my face ; that I
May pour for thee this golden wine, brim-high,
 Till round the glass thy fingers glow like gold.
 We 'll drown all hours : thy song, while hours are toll'd,
Shall leap, as fountains veil the changing sky.

Now kiss, and think that there are really those,
 My own high-bosomed beauty, who increase
  Vain gold, vain lore, and yet might choose our way !
  Through many years they toil ; then on a day
 They die not, — for their life was death, — but cease ;
And round their narrow lips the mould falls close.

WATCH thou and fear ; to-morrow thou shalt die.
   Or art thou sure thou shalt have time for death ?
   Is not the day which God's word promiseth
To come man knows not when ? In yonder sky,
Now while we speak, the sun speeds forth : can I
   Or thou assure him of his goal ?   God's breath
   Even at this moment haply quickeneth
The air to a flame ; till spirits, always nigh
Though screened and hid, shall walk the daylight here.
   And dost thou prate of all that man shall do ?
      Canst thou, who hast but plagues, presume to be
      Glad in his gladness that comes after thee ?
   Will *his* strength slay *thy* worm in Hell ? Go to :
Cover thy countenance, and watch, and fear.

III.

THINK thou and act; to-morrow thou shalt die.
  Outstretched in the sun's warmth upon the shore,
  Thou say'st : " Man's measured path is all gone o'er :
Up all his years, steeply, with strain and sigh,
Man clomb until he touched the truth ; and I,
  Even I, am he whom it was destined for."
  How should this be ? Art thou then so much more
Than they who sowed, that thou shouldst reap thereby ?

Nay, come up hither. From this wave-washed mound
  Unto the furthest flood-brim look with me ;
Then reach on with thy thought till it be drown'd.
  Miles and miles distant though the last line be,
And though thy soul sail leagues and leagues beyond, —
  Still, leagues beyond those leagues, there is more sea.

SONNETS LXXIV., .LXXV., LXXVI.

OLD AND NEW ART.

I. St. Luke the Painter.

GIVE honor unto Luke Evangelist ;
   For he it was (the aged legends say)
   Who first taught Art to fold her hands and pray.
Scarcely at once she dared to rend the mist
Of devious symbols : but soon having wist
   How sky-breadth and field-silence and this day
   Are symbols also in some deeper way,
She looked through these to God and was God's priest.

And if, past noon, her toil began to irk,
   And she sought talismans, and turned in vain
    To soulless self-reflections of man's skill, —
    Yet now, in this the twilight, she might still
   Kneel in the latter grass to pray again,
Ere the night cometh and she may not work.

II. Not as These.

"I am not as these are," the poet saith
   In youth's pride, and the painter, among men
   At bay, where never pencil comes nor pen,
And shut about with his own frozen breath.
To others, for whom only rhyme wins faith
   As poets, — only paint as painters, — then
   He turns in the cold silence; and again
Shrinking, "I am not as these are," he saith.

And say that this is so, what follows it?
   For were thine eyes set backwards in thine head,
    Such words were well; but they see on, and far.
Unto the lights of the great Past, new-lit
   Fair for the Future's track, look thou instead, —
    Say thou instead, "I am not as *these* are."

III. THE HUSBANDMEN.

THOUGH God, as one that is an householder,
  Called these to labor in his vineyard first,
  Before the husk of darkness was well burst
Bidding them grope their way out and bestir,
(Who, questioned of their wages, answered, " Sir,
  Unto each man a penny : ") though the worst
  Burthen of heat was theirs and the dry thirst :
Though God hath since found none such as these were
To do their work like them : — Because of this
  Stand not ye idle in the market-place.
    Which of ye knoweth *he* is not that last
Who may be first by faith and will? — yea, his
  The hand which after the appointed days
    And hours shall give a Future to their Past?

SONNET LXXVII.

SOUL'S BEAUTY.

UNDER the arch of Life, where love and death,
　　Terror and mystery, guard her shrine, I saw
　　Beauty enthroned ; and though her gaze struck awe,
I drew it in as simply as my breath.
Hers are the eyes which, over and beneath,
　　The sky and sea bend on thee, — which can draw,
　　By sea or sky or woman, to one law,
The allotted bondman of her palm and wreath.

This is that Lady Beauty, in whose praise
　　Thy voice and hand shake still, — long known to thee
　　　By flying hair and fluttering hem, — the beat
　　　Following her daily of thy heart and feet,
　　How passionately and irretrievably,
In what fond flight, how many ways and days !

SONNET LXXVIII.

.

BODY'S BEAUTY.

Of Adam's first wife, Lilith, it is told
   (The witch he loved before the gift of Eve,)
   That, ere the snake's, her sweet tongue could deceive,
And her enchanted hair was the first gold.
And still she sits, young while the earth is old,
   And, subtly of herself contemplative,
   Draws men to watch the bright web she can weave,
Till heart and body and life are in its hold.

The rose and poppy are her flowers ; for where
   Is he not found, O Lilith, whom shed scent
And soft-shed kisses and soft sleep shall snare?
   Lo ! as that youth's eyes burned at thine, so went
   Thy spell through him, and left his straight neck bent
And round his heart one strangling golden hair.

SONNET LXXIX.

THE MONOCHORD.

Is it this sky's vast vault or ocean's sound
    That is Life's self and draws my life from me,
    And by instinct ineffable decree
Holds my breath quailing on the bitter bound?
Nay, is it Life or Death, thus thunder-crown'd,
    That 'mid the tide of all emergency
    Now notes my separate wave, and to what sea
Its difficult eddies labor in the ground?

Oh ! what is this that knows the road I came,
The flame turned cloud, the cloud returned to flame,
    The lifted shifted steeps and all the way?—
That draws round me at last this wind-warm space,
And in regenerate rapture turns my face
    Upon the devious coverts of dismay?

SONNET LXXX.

FROM DAWN TO NOON.

As the child knows not if his mother's face
   Be fair ; nor of his elders yet can deem
   What each most is ; but as of hill or stream
At dawn, all glimmering life surrounds his place :
Who yet, tow'rd noon of his half-weary race,
   Pausing awhile beneath the high sun-beam
   And gazing steadily back, — as through a dream,
In things long past new features now can trace : —

Even so the thought that is at length fullgrown
   Turns back to note the sun-smit paths, all gray
And marvellous once, where first it walked alone ;
   And haply doubts, amid the unblenching day,
   Which most or least impelled its onward way, —
Those unknown things or these things overknown.

SONNET LXXXI.

MEMORIAL THRESHOLDS.

WHAT place so strange, — though unrevealèd snow
　With unimaginable fires arise
　At the earth's end, — what passion of surprise
Like frost-bound fire-girt scenes of long ago?
Lo ! this is none but I this hour ; and lo !
　This is the very place which to mine eyes
　Those mortal hours in vain immortalize,
'Mid hurrying crowds, with what alone I know.

City, of thine a single simple door,
　By some new Power reduplicate, must be
　Even yet my life-porch in eternity,
Even with one presence filled, as once of yore :
Or mocking winds whirl round a chaff-strown floor
　Thee and thy years and these my words and me.

SONNET LXXXII.

HOARDED JOY.

I SAID : " Nay, pluck not, — let the first fruit be :
　　Even as thou sayest, it is sweet and red,
　　But let it ripen still.　The tree's bent head
Sees in the stream its own fecundity
And bides the day of fulness.　Shall not we
　　At the sun's hour that day possess the shade,
　　And claim our fruit before its ripeness fade,
And eat it from the branch and praise the tree ? "

I say : " Alas ! our fruit hath wooed the sun
　　Too long, — 't is fallen and floats adown the stream.
Lo, the last clusters ! Pluck them every one,
　　And let us sup with summer ; ere the gleam
Of autumn set the year's pent sorrow free,
And the woods wail like echoes from the sea."

SONNET LXXXIII.

BARREN SPRING.

ONCE more the changed year's turning wheel returns :
   And as a girl sails balanced in the wind,
   And now before and now again behind
Stoops as it swoops, with cheek that laughs and burns, —
So Spring comes merry towards me here, but earns
   No answering smile from me, whose life is twin'd
   With the dead boughs that winter still must bind,
And whom to-day the Spring no more concerns.

Behold, this crocus is a withering flame ;
   This snowdrop, snow ; this apple-blossom's part
   To breed the fruit that breeds the serpent's art.
Nay, for these Spring-flowers, turn thy face from them,
Nor stay till on the year's last lily-stem
   The white cup shrivels round the golden heart.

SONNET LXXXIV.

FAREWELL TO THE GLEN.

SWEET stream-fed glen, why say " farewell " to thee
　　Who far'st so well and find'st for ever smooth
　　The brow of Time where man may read no ruth?
Nay, do thou rather say " farewell " to me,
Who now fare forth in bitterer fantasy
　　Than erst was mine where other shade might soothe
　　By other streams, what while in fragrant youth
The bliss of being sad made melancholy.

And yet, farewell ! For better shalt thou fare
　　When children bathe sweet faces in thy flow
And happy lovers blend sweet shadows there
　　In hours to come, than when an hour ago
Thine echoes had but one man's sighs to bear
　　And thy trees whispered what he feared to know.

SONNET LXXXV.

VAIN VIRTUES.

WHAT is the sorriest thing that enters Hell?
  None of the sins, — but this and that fair deed
  Which a soul's sin at length could supersede.
These yet are virgins, whom death's timely knell
Might once have sainted; whom the fiends compel
  Together now, in snake-bound shuddering sheaves
  Of anguish, while the pit's pollution leaves
Their refuse maidenhood abominable.

Night sucks them down, the tribute of the pit,
  Whose names, half entered in the book of Life,
  Were God's desire at noon.   And as their hair
And eyes sink last, the Torturer deigns no whit
  To gaze, but, yearning, waits his destined wife,
  The Sin still blithe on earth that sent them there.

SONNET LXXXVI.

LOST DAYS.

THE lost days of my life until to-day,
   What were they, could I see them on the street
   Lie as they fell? Would they be ears of wheat
Sown once for food but trodden into clay?
Or golden coins squandered and still to pay?
   Or drops of blood dabbling the guilty feet?
   Or such spilt water as in dreams must cheat
The undying throats of Hell, athirst alway?

I do not see them here; but after death
   God knows I know the faces I shall see,
Each one a murdered self, with low last breath.
   " I am thyself, — what hast thou done to me?"
" And I — and I — thyself," (lo ! each one saith,)
   " And thou thyself to all eternity !"

SONNET LXXXVII.

DEATH'S SONGSTERS.

WHEN first that horse, within whose populous womb
   The birth was death, o'ershadowed Troy with fate,
   Her elders, dubious of its Grecian freight,
Brought Helen there to sing the songs of home ;
She whispered, " Friends, I am alone ; come, come ! "
   Then, crouched within, Ulysses waxed afraid,
   And on his comrades' quivering mouths he laid
His hands, and held them till the voice was dumb.

The same was he who, lashed to his own mast,
   There where the sea-flowers screen the charnel-caves,
Beside the sirens' singing island pass'd,
   Till sweetness failed along the inveterate waves. . . .
Say, soul, — are songs of Death no heaven to thee,
Nor shames her lip the cheek of Victory ?

SONNET LXXXVIII.

HERO'S LAMP.[1]

THAT lamp thou fill'st in Eros' name to-night,
   O Hero, shall the Sestian augurs take
   To-morrow, and for drowned Leander's sake
To Anteros its fireless lip shall plight.
Aye, waft the unspoken vow : yet dawn's first light
   On ebbing storm and life twice ebb'd must break ;
   While 'neath no sunrise, by the Avernian Lake,
Lo where Love walks, Death's pallid neophyte.

That lamp within Anteros' shadowy shrine
   Shall stand unlit (for so the gods decree)
   Till some one man the happy issue see
Of a life's love, and bid its flame to shine :
Which still may rest unfir'd ; for, theirs or thine,
   O brother, what brought love to them or thee ?

---

[1] After the deaths of Leander and of Hero, the signal-lamp was dedicated to Anteros, with the edict that no man should light it unless his love had proved fortunate.

SONNET LXXXIX.

THE TREES OF THE GARDEN.

YE who have passed Death's haggard hills ; and ye
   Whom trees that knew your sires shall cease to know
   And still stand silent : — is it all a show, —
A wisp that laughs upon the wall? — decree
Of some inexorable supremacy
   Which ever, as man strains his blind surmise
   From depth to ominous depth, looks past his eyes,
Sphinx-faced with unabashéd augury ?

Nay, rather question the Earth's self.   Invoke
   The storm-felled forest-trees moss-grown to-day
   Whose roots are hillocks where the children play ;
Or ask the silver sapling 'neath what yoke
   Those stars, his spray-crown's clustering gems, shall
      wage
   Their journey still when his boughs shrink with age.

SONNET XC.

"RETRO ME, SATHANA!"

GET thee behind me.   Even as, heavy-curled,
   Stooping against the wind, a charioteer
   Is snatched from out his chariot by the hair,
So shall Time be ; and as the void car, hurled
Abroad by reinless steeds, even so the world :
   Yea, even as chariot-dust upon the air,
   It shall be sought and not found anywhere.
Get thee behind me, Satan.   Oft unfurled,
Thy perilous wings can beat and break like lath
   Much mightiness of men to win thee praise.
   Leave these weak feet to tread in narrow ways.
Thou still, upon the broad vine-sheltered path,
Mayst wait the turning of the phials of wrath
   For certain years, for certain months and days.

SONNET XCI.

LOST ON BOTH SIDES.

As when two men have loved a woman well,
　　Each hating each, through Love's and Death's deceit ;
　　Since not for either this stark marriage-sheet
And the long pauses of this wedding-bell ;
Yet o'er her grave the night and day dispel
　　At last their feud forlorn, with cold and heat ;
　　Nor other than dear friends to death may fleet
The two lives left that most of her can tell : —

So separate hopes, which in a soul had wooed
　　The one same Peace, strove with each other long,
　　And Peace before their faces perished since :
So through that soul, in restless brotherhood,
　　They roam together now, and wind among
　　Its bye-streets, knocking at the dusty inns.

SONNETS XCII., XCIII.

THE SUN'S SHAME.

I.

BEHOLDING youth and hope in mockery caught
   From life ; and mocking pulses that remain
   When the soul's death of bodily death is fain ;
Honor unknown, and honor known unsought ;
And penury's sedulous self-torturing thought
   On gold, whose master therewith buys his bane ;
   And longed-for woman longing all in vain
For lonely man with love's desire distraught ;
And wealth, and strength, and power, and pleasantness,
   Given unto bodies of whose souls men say,
   None poor and weak, slavish and foul, as they : —
Beholding these things, I behold no less
The blushing morn and blushing eve confess
   The shame that loads the intolerable day.

II.

As some true chief of men, bowed down with stress
   Of life's disastrous eld, on blossoming youth
   May gaze, and murmur with self-pity and ruth, —
" Might I thy fruitless treasure but possess,
Such blessing of mine all coming years should bless ; " —
   Then sends one sigh forth to the unknown goal,
   And bitterly feels breathe against his soul
The hour swift-winged of nearer nothingness : —

Even so the World's gray Soul to the green World
   Perchance one hour must cry : " Woe 's me, for whom
   Inveteracy of ill portends the doom, —
Whose heart's old fire in shadow of shame is furl'd :
   While thou even as of yore art journeying,
   All soulless now, yet merry with the Spring ! "

SONNET XCIV.

MICHELANGELO'S KISS.

GREAT Michelangelo, with age grown bleak
    And uttermost labors, having once o'ersaid
    All grievous memories on his long life shed,
This worst regret to one true heart could speak : —
That when, with sorrowing love and reverence meek,
    He stooped o'er sweet Colonna's dying bed,
    His Muse and dominant Lady, spirit-wed, —
Her hand he kissed, but not her brow or cheek.

O Buonarruoti, — good at Art's fire-wheels
    To urge her chariot ! — even thus the Soul,
    Touching at length some sorely-chastened goal,
Earns oftenest but a little : her appeals
    Were deep and mute, — lowly her claim.   Let be :
    What holds for her Death's garner ?   And for thee ?

SONNET XCV.

THE VASE OF LIFE.

AROUND the vase of Life at your slow pace
   He has not crept, but turned it with his hands,
   And all its sides already understands.
There, girt, one breathes alert for some great race ;
Whose road runs far by sands and fruitful space ;
   Who laughs, yet through the jolly throng has pass'd ;
   Who weeps, nor stays for weeping ; who at last,
A youth, stands somewhere crowned, with silent face.

And he has filled this vase with wine for blood,
   With blood for tears, with spice for burning vow,
     With watered flowers for buried love most fit ;
And would have cast it shattered to the flood,
   Yet in Fate's name has kept it whole ; which now
     Stands empty till his ashes fall in it.

SONNET XCVI.

LIFE THE BELOVED.

As thy friend's face, with shadow of soul o'erspread,
　　Somewhile unto thy sight perchance hath been
　　Ghastly and strange, yet never so is seen
In thought, but to all fortunate favor wed ;
As thy love's death-bound features never dead
　　To memory's glass return, but contravene
　　Frail fugitive days, and alway keep, I ween,
Than all new life a livelier lovelihead : —

So Life herself, thy spirit's friend and love,
　　Even still as Spring's authentic harbinger
　　　Glows with fresh hours for hope to glorify ;
Though pale she lay when in the winter grove
　　Her funeral flowers were snow-flakes shed on her
　　　And the red wings of frost-fire rent the sky.

SONNET XCVII.

A SUPERSCRIPTION.

Look in my face ; my name is Might-have-been ;
  I am also called No-more, Too-late, Farewell ;
  Unto thine ear I hold the dead-sea shell
Cast up thy Life's foam-fretted feet between ;
Unto thine eyes the glass where that is seen
  Which had Life's form and Love's, but by my spell
  Is now a shaken shadow intolerable,
Of ultimate things unuttered the frail screen.

Mark me, how still I am ! But should there dart
  One moment through thy soul the soft surprise
  Of that winged Peace which lulls the breath of sighs, —
Then shalt thou see me smile, and turn apart
Thy visage to mine ambush at thy heart
  Sleepless with cold commemorative eyes.

HE AND I.

WHENCE came his feet into my field, and why?
    How is it that he sees it all so drear?
    How do I see his seeing, and how hear
The name his bitter silence knows it by?
This was the little fold of separate sky
    Whose pasturing clouds in the soul's atmosphere
    Drew living light from one continual year:
How should he find it lifeless?   He, or I?

Lo! this new Self now wanders round my field,
    With plaints for every flower, and for each tree
    A moan, the sighing wind's auxiliary:
And o'er sweet waters of my life, that yield
Unto his lips no draught but tears unseal'd,
    Even in my place he weeps.   Even I, not he.

SONNETS XCIX., C.

NEWBORN DEATH.

I.

To-DAY Death seems to me an infant child
    Which her worn mother Life upon my knee
    Has set to grow my friend and play with me ;
If haply so my heart might be beguil'd
To find no terrors in a face so mild, —
    If haply so my weary heart might be
    Unto the newborn milky eyes of thee,
O Death, before resentment reconcil'd.

How long, O Death ? And shall thy feet depart
    Still a young child's with mine, or wilt thou stand
Fullgrown the helpful daughter of my heart,
    What time with thee indeed I reach the strand
Of the pale wave which knows thee what thou art,
    And drink it in the hollow of thy hand ?

AND thou, O Life, the lady of all bliss,
  With whom, when our first heart beat full and fast,
  I wandered till the haunts of men were pass'd,
And in fair places found all bowers amiss
Till only woods and waves might hear our kiss,
  While to the winds all thought of Death we cast : —
  Ah, Life ! and must I have from thee at last
No smile to greet me and no babe but this?

Lo ! Love, the child once ours ; and Song, whose hair
  Blew like a flame and blossomed like a wreath ;
And Art, whose eyes were worlds by God found fair ;
  These o'er the book of Nature mixed their breath
With neck-twined arms, as oft we watched them there :
  And did these die that thou mightst bear me Death?

SONNET CI.

THE ONE HOPE.

WHEN vain desire at last and vain regret
    Go hand in hand to death, and all is vain,
    What shall assuage the unforgotten pain
And teach the unforgetful to forget?
Shall Peace be still a sunk stream long unmet, —
    Or may the soul at once in a green plain
    Stoop through the spray of some sweet life-fountain
And cull the dew-drenched flowering amulet?

Ah ! when the wan soul in that golden air
    Between the scriptured petals softly blown
    Peers breathless for the gift of grace unknown, —
Ah ! let none other alien spell soe'er
But only the one Hope's one name be there, —
    Not less nor more, but even that word alone.

LYRICS,

&c.

SOOTHSAY.

LET no man ask thee of anything
Not yearborn between Spring and Spring.
More of all worlds than he can know,
Each day the single sun doth show.
A trustier gloss than thou canst give
From all wise scrolls demonstrative,
The sea doth sigh and the wind sing.

Let no man awe thee on any height
Of earthly kingship's mouldering might.
The dust his heel holds meet for thy brow
Hath all of it been what both are now;
And thou and he may plague together
A beggar's eyes in some dusty weather
When none that is now knows sound or sight.

Crave thou no dower of earthly things
Unworthy Hope's imaginings.
To have brought true birth of Song to be
And to have won hearts to Poesy,
Or anywhere in the sun or rain
To have loved and been beloved again,
Is loftiest reach of Hope's bright wings.

The wild waifs cast up by the sea
Are diverse ever seasonably.
Even so the soul-tides still may land
A different drift upon the sand.
But one the sea is evermore :
And one be still, 'twixt shore and shore,
As the sea's life, thy soul in thee.

Say, hast thou pride?　How then may fit
Thy mood with flatterers' silk-spun wit?
Haply the sweet voice lifts thy crest,
A breeze of fame made manifest.
Nay, but then chaf'st at flattery?　Pause :
Be sure thy wrath is not because
It makes thee feel thou lovest it.

Let thy soul strive that still the same
Be early friendship's sacred flame.
The affinities have strongest part
In youth, and draw men heart to heart :
As life wears on and finds no rest,
The individual in each breast
Is tyrannous to sunder them.

In the life-drama's stern cue-call,
A friend 's a part well-prized by all :
And if thou meet an enemy,
What art thou that none such should be ?
Even so : but if the two parts run
Into each other and grow one,
Then comes the curtain's cue to fall.

Whate'er by other's need is claimed
More than by thine, — to him unblamed
Resign it : and if he should hold
What more than he thou lack'st, bread, gold,
Or any good whereby we live, —
To thee such substance let him give
Freely : nor he nor thou be shamed.

Strive that thy works prove equal : lest
That work which thou hast done the best
Should come to be to thee at length
(Even as to envy seems the strength
Of others) hateful and abhorr'd, —
Thine own above thyself made lord, —
Of self-rebuke the bitterest.

Unto the man of yearning thought
And aspiration, to do nought
Is in itself almost an act, —
Being chasm-fire and cataract
Of the soul's utter depths unseal'd.
Yet woe to thee if once thou yield
Unto the act of doing nought !

How callous seems beyond revoke
The clock with its last listless stroke !
How much too late at length ! — to trace
The hour on its forewarning face,
The thing thou hast not dared to do ! . . . .
Behold, this *may* be thus !   Ere true
It prove, arise and bear thy yoke.

Let lore of all Theology
Be to thy soul what it *can* be :
But know, — the Power that fashions man
Measured not out thy little span
For thee to take the meting-rod
In turn, and so approve on God
Thy science of Theometry.

To God at best, to Chance at worst,
Give thanks for good things, last as first.
But windstrown blossom is that good
Whose apple is not gratitude.
Even if no prayer uplift thy face,
Let the sweet right to render grace
As thy soul's cherished child be nurs'd.

Didst ever say, "Lo, I forget"?
Such thought was to remember yet.
As in a gravegarth, count to see
The monuments of memory.
Be this thy soul's appointed scope : —
Gaze onward without claim to hope,
Nor, gazing backward, court regret.

CHIMES.

I.

Honey-flowers to the honey-comb
And the honey-bees from home.

A honey-comb and a honey-flower,
And the bee shall have his hour.

A honeyed heart for the honey-comb,
And the humming bee flies home.

A heavy heart in the honey-flower,
And the bee has had his hour.

II.

A honey-cell 's in the honeysuckle,
And the honey-bee knows it well.

The honey-comb has a heart of honey,
And the humming bee 's so bonny.

A honey-flower 's the honeysuckle,
And the bee 's in the honey-bell.

The honeysuckle is sucked of honey,
And the bee is heavy and bonny.

III.

Brown shell first for the butterfly
And a bright wing by and by.

Butterfly, good-bye to your shell,
And, bright wings, speed you well.

Bright lamplight for the butterfly
And a burnt wing by and by.

Butterfly, alas for your shell,
And, bright wings, fare you well.

IV.

Lost love-labor and lullaby,
And lowly let love lie.

Lost love-morrow and love-fellow
And love's life lying low.

Lovelorn labor and life laid by
And lowly let love lie.

Late love-longing and life-sorrow
And love's life lying low.

v.

Beauty's body and benison
With a bosom-flower new-blown.

Bitter beauty and blessing bann'd
With a breast to burn and brand.

Beauty's bower in the dust o'erblown
With a bare white breast of bone.

Barren beauty and bower of sand
With a blast on either hand.

.

VI.

Buried bars in the breakwater
And bubble of the brimming weir.

Body's blood in the breakwater
And a buried body's bier.

Buried bones in the breakwater
And bubble of the brawling weir.

Bitter tears in the breakwater
And a breaking heart to bear.

VII.

Hollow heaven and the hurricane
And hurry of the heavy rain.

Hurried clouds in the hollow heaven
And a heavy rain hard-driven.

The heavy rain it hurries amain
And heaven and the hurricane.

Hurrying wind o'er the heaven's hollow
And the heavy rain to follow.

PARTED PRESENCE.

LOVE, I speak to your heart,
  Your heart that is always here.
  Oh draw me deep to its sphere,
Though you and I are apart ;
And yield, by the spirit's art,
  Each distant gift that is dear.
  O love, my love, you are here !

.

Your eyes are afar to-day,
  Yet, love, look now in mine eyes.
  Two hearts sent forth may despise
All dead things by the way.
All between is decay,
  Dead hours and this hour that dies,
  O love, look deep in mine eyes !

Your hands to-day are not here,
　Yet lay them, love, in my hands.
　The hourglass sheds its sands
All day for the dead hours' bier ;
But now, as two hearts draw near,
　This hour like a flower expands.
　O love, your hands in my hands !

Your voice is not on the air,
　Yet, love, I can hear your voice :
　It bids my heart to rejoice
As knowing your heart is there, —
A music sweet to declare
　The truth of your steadfast choice.
　O love, how sweet is your voice !
　　　　　·

To-day your lips are afar,
　Yet draw my lips to them, love.
　Around, beneath, and above,
Is frost to bind and to bar ;
But where I am and you are,
　Desire and the fire thereof.
　O kiss me, kiss me, my love !

Your heart is never away,
    But ever with mine, for ever,
    For ever without endeavor,
To-morrow, love, as to-day ;
Two blent hearts never astray,
    Two souls no power may sever,
    Together, O my love, for ever !

A DEATH-PARTING.

LEAVES and rain and the days of the year,
  (*Water-willow and wellaway,*)
All these fall, and my soul gives ear,
And she is hence who once was here.
  (*With a wind blown night and day.*)

Ah! but now, for a secret sign,
  (*The willow's wan and the water white,*)
In the held breath of the day's decline
Her very face seemed pressed to mine.
  (*With a wind blown day and night.*)

O love, of my death my life is fain;
  (*The willows wave on the water-way,*)
Your cheek and mine are cold in the rain,
But warm they 'll be when we meet again.
  (*With a wind blown night and day.*)

Mists are heaved and cover the sky;
   (*The willows wail in the waning light,*)
O loose your lips, leave space for a sigh, —
They seal my soul, I cannot die.
   (*With a wind blown day and night.*)

Leaves and rain and the days of the year,
   (*Water-willow and wellaway,*)
All still fall, and I still give ear,
And she is hence, and I am here.
   (*With a wind blown night and day.*)

SPHERAL CHANGE.

In this new shade of Death, the show
    Passes me still of form and face ;
Some bent, some gazing as they go,
    Some swiftly, some at a dull pace,
    Not one that speaks in any case.

If only one might speak ! — the one
    Who never waits till I come near ;
But always seated all alone
    As listening to the sunken air,
    Is gone before I come to her.

O dearest ! while we lived and died
    A living death in every day,
Some hours we still were side by side,
    When where I was you too might stay
    And rest and need not go away.

O nearest, furthest ! Can there be
  At length some hard-earned heart-won home,
Where, — exile changed for sanctuary, —
  Our lot may fill indeed its sum,
  And you may wait and I may come?

10

SUNSET WINGS.

To-night this sunset spreads two golden wings
    Cleaving the western sky;
Winged too with wind it is, and winnowings
Of birds; as if the day's last hour in rings
    Of strenuous flight must die.

Sun-steeped in fire, the homeward pinions sway
    Above the dovecote-tops;
And clouds of starlings, ere they rest with day,
Sink, clamorous like mill-waters, at wild play,
    By turns in every copse:

Each tree heart-deep the wrangling rout receives, —
    Save for the whirr within,
You could not tell the starlings from the leaves;
Then one great puff of wings, and the swarm heaves
    Away with all its din.

Even thus Hope's hours, in ever-eddying flight,
 To many a refuge tend ;
With the first light she laughed, and the last light
Glows round her still ; who natheless in the night
 At length must make an end.

And now the mustering rooks innumerable
 Together sail and soar,
While for the day's death, like a tolling knell,
Unto the heart they seem to cry, Farewell,
 No more, farewell, no more !

Is Hope not plumed, as 't were a fiery dart ?
 And oh ! thou dying day,
Even as thou goest must she too depart,
And Sorrow fold such pinions on the heart
 As will not fly away ?

.

SONG AND MUSIC.

O LEAVE your hand where it lies cool
   Upon the eyes whose lids are hot :
Its rosy shade is bountiful
   Of silence, and assuages thought.
O lay your lips against your hand
   And let me feel your breath through it,
While through the sense your song shall fit
   The soul to understand.

The music lives upon my brain
   Between your hands within mine eyes ;
It stirs your lifted throat like pain,
   An aching pulse of melodies.
Lean nearer, let the music pause :
   The soul may better understand
Your music, shadowed in your hand,
   Now while the song withdraws.

THREE SHADOWS.

I LOOKED and saw your eyes
   In the shadow of your hair,
As a traveller sees the stream
   In the shadow of the wood ;
And I said, " My faint heart sighs,
   Ah me ! to linger there,
To drink deep and to dream
   In that sweet solitude."

I looked and saw your heart
   In the shadow of your eyes,
As a seeker sees the gold
   In the shadow of the stream ;
And I said, " Ah me ! what art
   Should win the immortal prize,
Whose want must make life cold
   And Heaven a hollow dream ? "

I looked and saw your love
  In the shadow of your heart,
As a diver sees the pearl
  In the shadow of the sea ;
And I murmured, not above
  My breath, but all apart, —
" Ah ! you can love, true girl,
  And is your love for me ? "

ALAS, SO LONG!

Ah! dear one, we were young so long,
  It seemed that youth would never go,
For skies and trees were ever in song
  And water in singing flow
In the days we never again shall know.
      Alas, so long!
   Ah! then was it all Spring weather?
   Nay, but we were young and together.

Ah! dear one, I 've been old so long,
  It seems that age is loth to part,
Though days and years have never a song,
  And oh! have they still the art
That warmed the pulses of heart to heart?
      Alas, so long!
   Ah! then was it all Spring weather?
   Nay, but we were young and together.

Ah ! dear one, you 've been dead so long, —
　How long until we meet again,
Where hours may never lose their song
　Nor flowers forget the rain
In glad noonlight that never shall wane ?
　　　Alas, so long !
　　Ah ! shall it be then Spring weather,
　　And ah ! shall we be young together ?

ADIEU.

WAVING whispering trees,
What do you say to the breeze
   And what says the breeze to you?
'Mid passing souls ill at ease,
Moving murmuring trees,
   Would ye ever wave an Adieu

Tossing turbulent seas,
Winds that wrestle with these,
   Echo heard in the shell, —
'Mid fleeting life ill at ease,
Restless ravening seas, —
   Would the echo sigh Farewell?

Surging sumptuous skies,
For ever a new surprise,
   Clouds eternally new, —

Is every flake that flies,
Widening wandering skies,
   For a sign — Farewell, Adieu?

Sinking suffering heart
That know'st how weary thou art, —
   Soul so fain for a flight, —
Aye, spread your wings to depart,
Sad soul and sorrowing heart, —
   Adieu, Farewell, Good-night.

INSOMNIA.

Thin are the night-skirts left behind
　By daybreak hours that onward creep,
　And thin, alas ! the shred of sleep
That wavers with the spirit's wind :
But in half-dreams that shift and roll
　And still remember and forget,
My soul this hour has drawn your soul
　　A little nearer yet.

Our lives, most dear, are never near,
　Our thoughts are never far apart,
　Though all that draws us heart to heart
Seems fainter now and now more clear.
To-night Love claims his full control,
　And with desire and with regret
My soul this hour has drawn your soul
　　A little nearer yet.

Is there a home where heavy earth
    Melts to bright air that breathes no pain,
    Where water leaves no thirst again
And springing fire is Love's new birth?
If faith long bound to one true goal
    May there at length its hope beget,
My soul that hour shall draw your soul
    For ever nearer yet.

POSSESSION.

THERE is a cloud above the sunset hill,
 That wends and makes no stay,
For its goal lies beyond the fiery west ;
A lingering breath no calm can chase away,
The onward labor of the wind's last will ;
A flying foam that overleaps the crest
Of the top wave : and in possession still
A further reach of longing ; though at rest
 From all the yearning years,
Together in the bosom of that day
Ye cling, and with your kisses drink your tears.

THE CLOUD CONFINES.

THE day is dark and the night
  To him that would search their heart ;
  No lips of cloud that will part
Nor morning song in the light :
  Only, gazing alone,
  To him wild shadows are shown,
  Deep under deep unknown
And height above unknown height.
      Still we say as we go, —
        " Strange to think by the way,
      Whatever there is to know,
        That shall we know one day."

The Past is over and fled ;
  Named new, we name it the old ;
  Thereof some tale hath been told,
But no word comes from the dead ;

Whether at all they be,
Or whether as bond or free,
Or whether they too were we,
Or by what spell they have sped.
    Still we say as we go, —
        " Strange to think by the way,
      Whatever there is to know,
        That shall we know one day."

What of the heart of hate
    That beats in thy breast, O Time? —
    Red strife from the furthest prime,
And anguish of fierce debate ;
    War that shatters her slain,
    And peace that grinds them as grain,
    And eyes fixed ever in vain
On the pitiless eyes of Fate.
    Still we say as we go, —
        " Strange to think by the way,
      Whatever there is to know,
        That shall we know one day."

What of the heart of love
    That bleeds in thy breast, O Man? —

Thy kisses snatched 'neath the ban
Of fangs that mock them above ;
Thy bells prolonged unto knells,
Thy hope that a breath dispels,
Thy bitter forlorn farewells
And the empty echoes thereof?
Still we say as we go, —
"Strange to think by the way,
Whatever there is to know,
That shall we know one day."

The sky leans dumb on the sea,
Aweary with all its wings ;
And oh ! the song the sea sings
Is dark everlastingly.
Our past is clean forgot,
Our present is and is not,
Our future 's a sealed seedplot,
And what betwixt them are we? —
We who say as we go, —
"Strange to think by the way,
Whatever there is to know,
That shall we know one day."

SONNETS.

17

FOR

THE HOLY FAMILY,

BY MICHELANGELO.

(*In the National Gallery.*[1])

TURN not the prophet's page, O Son !   He knew
   All that thou hast to suffer, and hath writ.
   Not yet thine hour of knowledge.   Infinite
The sorrows that thy manhood's lot must rue
And dire acquaintance of thy grief.   That clue
     The spirits of thy mournful ministerings
     Seek through yon scroll in silence.   For these things
The angels have desired to look into.

Still before Eden waves the fiery sword, —
     Her Tree of Life unransomed : whose sad Tree
     Of Knowledge yet to growth of Calvary
       Must yield its Tempter, — Hell the earliest dead
Of Earth resign, — and yet, O Son and Lord,
     The Seed o' the woman bruise the serpent's head.

[1] In this picture the Virgin Mother is seen withholding from the
Child Saviour the prophetic writings in which his sufferings are
foretold.   Angelic figures beside them examine a scroll.

FOR

SPRING,

BY SANDRO BOTTICELLI.

(*In the Accademia of Florence.*)

WHAT masque of what old wind-withered New-Year
   Honors this Lady?[1]   Flora, wanton-eyed
   For birth, and with all flowrets prankt and pied :
Aurora, Zephyrus, with mutual cheer
Of clasp and kiss : the Graces circling near,
   'Neath bower-linked arch of white arms glorified :
   And with those feathered feet which hovering glide
O'er Spring's brief bloom, Hermes the harbinger.

Birth-bare, not death-bare yet, the young stems stand,
   This Lady's temple-columns : o'er her head
   Love wings his shaft.   What mystery here is read
Of homage or of hope?   But how command
   Dead Springs to answer?   And how question here
   These mummers of that wind-withered New-Year?

[1] The same lady, here surrounded by the masque of Spring, is
evidently the subject of a portrait by Botticelli formerly in the
Pourtalès collection in Paris.   This portrait is inscribed " Smer-
alda Bandinelli."

FIVE ENGLISH POETS.

I. THOMAS CHATTERTON.

WITH Shakspeare's manhood at a boy's wild heart, —
　　Through Hamlet's doubt to Shakspeare near allied,
　　And kin to Milton through his Satan's pride, —
At Death's sole door he stooped, and craved a dart ;
And to the dear new bower of England's art, — ·
　　Even to that shrine Time else had deified,
　　The unuttered heart that soared against his side, —
Drove the fell point, and smote life's seals apart.

Thy nested home-loves, noble Chatterton ;
　　The angel-trodden stair thy soul could trace
　　Up Redcliffe's spire ; and in the world's armed space
Thy gallant sword-play : — these to many an one
Are sweet for ever ; as thy grave unknown
　　And love-dream of thine unrecorded face.

II. WILLIAM BLAKE.

(To Frederick Shields, on his Sketch of Blake's work-room
and death-room, 3, Fountain Court, Strand.)

This is the place.   Even here the.dauntless soul,
 The unflinching hand, wrought on ; till in that nook,
 As on that very bed, his life partook
New birth, and passed.   Yon river's dusky shoal,
Whereto the close-built coiling lanes unroll,
 Faced his work-window, whence his eyes would stare,
 Thought-wandering, unto nought that met them there,
But to the unfettered irreversible goal.

This cupboard, Holy of Holies, held the cloud
 Of his soul writ and limned ; this other one,
His true wife's charge, full oft to their abode
 Yielded for daily bread the martyr's stone,
 Ere yet their food might be that Bread alone,
The words now home-speech of the mouth of God.

III. SAMUEL TAYLOR COLERIDGE.

His Soul fared forth (as from the deep home-grove
   The father-songster plies the hour-long quest,)
   To feed his soul-brood hungering in the nest ;
But his warm Heart, the mother-bird, above
Their callow fledgling progeny still hove
   With tented roof of wings and fostering breast
   Till the Soul fed the soul-brood.   Richly blest
From Heaven their growth, whose food was Human Love.

Yet ah !   Like desert pools that show the stars
   Once in long leagues, — even such the scarce-snatched
      hours
   Which deepening pain left to his lordliest powers : —
Heaven lost through spider-trammelled prison-bars.
   Six years, from sixty saved !   Yet kindling skies
   Own them, a beacon to our centuries.

IV. JOHN KEATS.

THE weltering London ways where children weep
    And girls whom none call maidens laugh, — strange
      road
    Miring his outward steps, who inly trode
The bright Castalian brink and Latmos' steep : —
Even such his life's cross-paths ; till deathly deep
    He toiled through sands of Lethe ; and long pain,
    Weary with labor spurned and love found vain,
In dead Rome's sheltering shadow wrapped his sleep.

O pang-dowered Poet, whose reverberant lips
And heart-strung lyre awoke the Moon's eclipse, —
    Thou whom the daisies glory in growing o'er, —
Their fragrance clings around thy name, not writ
But rumor'd in water, while the fame of it
    Along Time's flood goes echoing evermore.

V. PERCY BYSSHE SHELLEY.

(INSCRIPTION FOR THE COUCH, STILL PRESERVED, ON WHICH HE
PASSED THE LAST NIGHT OF HIS LIFE.)

'TWIXT those twin worlds, — the world of Sleep, which
    gave
  No dream to warn, — the tidal world of Death,
  Which the earth's sea, as the earth, replenisheth, —
Shelley, Song's orient sun, to breast the wave,
Rose from this couch that morn.   Ah ! did he brave
  Only the sea ? — or did man's deed of hell
  Engulph his bark 'mid mists impenetrable ? . . . .
No eye discerned, nor any power might save.

When that mist cleared, O Shelley ! what dread veil
  Was rent for thee, to whom far-darkling Truth
  Reigned sovereign guide through thy brief ageless
    youth ?
Was the Truth *thy* Truth, Shelley ? — Hush !   All-Hail,
  Past doubt, thou gav'st it ; and in Truth's bright sphere
  Art first of praisers, being most praisèd here.

TIBER, NILE, AND THAMES.

THE head and hands of murdered Cicero,
    Above his seat high in the Forum hung,
    Drew jeers and burning tears. When on the rung
Of a swift-mounted ladder, all aglow,
Fulvia, Mark Antony's shameless wife, with show
    Of foot firm-poised and gleaming arm upflung,
    Bade her sharp needle pierce that god-like tongue
Whose speech fed Rome even as the Tiber's flow.

And thou, Cleopatra's Needle, that hadst thrid
· Great skirts of Time ere she and Antony hid
    Dead hope ! — hast thou too reached, surviving death,
A city of sweet speech scorned, — on whose chill stone
Keats withered, Coleridge pined, and Chatterton,
    Breadless, with poison froze the God-fired breath ?

THE LAST THREE FROM TRAFALGAR

AT THE ANNIVERSARY BANQUET,
21ST OCTOBER, 187*.

In grappled ships around The Victory,
    Three boys did England's Duty with stout cheer,
    While one dread truth was kept from every ear,
More dire than deafening fire that churned the sea:
For in the flag-ship's weltering cockpit, he
    Who was the Battle's Heart without a peer,
    He who had seen all fearful sights save Fear,
Was passing from all life save Victory.

And round the old memorial board to-day,
    Three graybeards — each a warworn British Tar —
    View through the mist of years that hour afar:
Who soon shall greet, 'mid memories of fierce fray,
The impassioned soul which on its radiant way
    Soared through the fiery cloud of Trafalgar.

CZAR ALEXANDER THE SECOND.

(13TH MARCH, 1881.)

FROM him did forty million serfs, endow'd
    Each with six feet of death-due soil, receive
    Rich freeborn lifelong land, whereon to sheave
Their country's harvest.   These to-day aloud
Demand of Heaven a Father's blood, — sore bow'd
    With tears and thrilled with wrath; who, while they
        grieve,
    On every guilty head would fain achieve
All torment by his edicts disallow'd.

He stayed the knout's red-ravening fangs; and first
    Of Russian traitors, his own murderers go
    White to the tomb.   While he, — laid foully low
With limbs red-rent, with festering brain which erst
Willed kingly freedom, — 'gainst the deed accurst
    To God bears witness of his people's woe.

WORDS ON THE WINDOW-PANE.[1]

DID she in summer write it, or in spring,
  Or with this wail of autumn at her ears,
  Or in some winter left among old years
Scratched it through tettered cark? A certain thing
That round her heart the frost was hardening,
  Not to be thawed of tears, which on this pane
  Channelled the rime, perchance, in fevered rain,
For false man's sake and love's most bitter sting.

Howbeit, between this last word and the next
Unwritten, subtly seasoned was the smart,
  And here at least the grace to weep: if she,
Rather, midway in her disconsolate text,
Rebelled not, loathing from the trodden heart
  That thing which she had found man's love to be.

[1] For a woman's fragmentary inscription.

WINTER.

How large that thrush looks on the bare thorn-tree !
   A swarm of such, three little months ago,
   Had hidden in the leaves and let none know
Save by the outburst of their minstrelsy.
A white flake here and there — a snow-lily
   Of last night's frost — our naked flower-beds hold ;
   And for a rose-flower on the darkling mould
The hungry redbreast gleams.   No bloom, no bee.

The current shudders to its ice-bound sedge :
   Nipped in their bath, the stark reeds one by one
   Flash each its clinging diamond in the sun :
'Neath winds which for this Winter's sovereign pledge
Shall curb great king-masts to the ocean's edge
   And leave memorial forest-kings o'erthrown.

SPRING.

Soft–littered is the new-year's lambing-fold,
  And in the hollowed haystack at its side
  The shepherd lies o' nights now, wakeful-eyed
At the ewes' travailing call through the dark cold.
The young rooks cheep 'mid the thick caw o' the old :
  And near unpeopled stream-sides, on the ground,
  By her spring-cry the moorhen's nest is found,
Where the drained flood-lands flaunt their marigold.

Chill are the gusts to which the pastures cower,
  And chill the current where the young reeds stand
  As green and close as the young wheat on land :
Yet here the cuckoo and the cuckoo-flower
Plight to the heart Spring's perfect imminent hour
  Whose breath shall soothe you like your dear one's
    hand.

THE CHURCH-PORCH.

SISTER, first shake we off the dust we have
 Upon our feet, lest it defile the stones
 Inscriptured, covering their sacred bones
Who lie i' the aisles which keep the names they gave,
Their trust abiding round them in the grave;
 Whom painters paint for visible orisons,
 And to whom sculptors pray in stone and bronze;
Their voices echo still like a spent wave.

Without here, the church-bells are but a tune,
And on the carven church-door this hot noon
 Lays all its heavy sunshine here without:
But having entered in, we shall find there
Silence, and sudden dimness, and deep prayer,
 And faces of crowned angels all about.

UNTIMELY LOST.

(OLIVER MADOX BROWN. BORN 1855;
DIED 1874.)

UPON the landscape of his coming life
  A youth high-gifted gazed, and found it fair :
  The heights of work, the floods of praise, were there.
What friendships, what desires, what love, what wife ? —
All things to come.   The fanned springtide was rife
  With imminent solstice ; and the ardent air
  Had summer sweets and autumn fires to bear ; —
Heart's ease full-pulsed with perfect strength for strife.

A mist has risen : we see the youth no more :
  Does *he* see on and strive on?   And may we
  Late-tottering worldworn hence, find *his* to be
The young strong hand which helps us up that shore?
Or, echoing the No More with Nevermore,
  Must Night be ours and his?   We hope : and he?

PLACE DE LA BASTILLE, PARIS.

How dear the sky has been above this place !
　　Small treasures of this sky that we see here
　　Seen weak through prison-bars from year to year ;
Eyed with a painful prayer upon God's grace
To save, and tears that stayed along the face
　　Lifted at sunset.　Yea, how passing dear,
　　Those nights when through the bars a wind left clear
The heaven, and moonlight soothed the limpid space !

So was it, till one night the secret kept
　　Safe in low vault and stealthy corridor
　　　Was blown abroad on gospel-tongues of flame.
　O ways of God, mysterious evermore !
How many on this spot have cursed and wept
　　That all might stand here now and own Thy Name.

" FOUND."

(FOR A PICTURE.)

" THERE is a budding morrow in midnight : " —
  So sang our Keats, our English nightingale.
  And here, as lamps across the bridge turn pale
In London's smokeless resurrection-light,
Dark breaks to dawn. But o'er the deadly blight
  Of love deflowered and sorrow of none avail
  Which makes this man gasp and this woman quail,
Can day from darkness ever again take flight?

Ah ! gave not these two hearts their mutual pledge,
Under one mantle sheltered 'neath the hedge
  In gloaming courtship? And O God ! to-day
He only knows he holds her ; — but what part
Can life now take? She cries in her locked heart, —
  " Leave me — I do not know you — go away ! "

A SEA–SPELL.

(FOR A PICTURE.)

HER lute hangs shadowed in the apple-tree,
    While flashing fingers weave the sweet-strung spell
    Between its chords ; and as the wild notes swell,
The sea-bird for those branches leaves the sea.
But to what sound her listening ear stoops she?
    What netherworld gulf-whispers doth she hear,
    In answering echoes from what planisphere,
Along the wind, along the estuary?

She sinks into her spell : and when full soon
    Her lips move and she soars into her song,
    What creatures of the midmost main shall throng
In furrowed surf-clouds to the summoning rune :
    Till he, the fated mariner, hears her cry,
    And up her rock, bare-breasted, comes to die?

FIAMMETTA.

(FOR A PICTURE.)

BEHOLD Fiammetta, shown in Vision here.
   Gloom-girt 'mid Spring-flushed apple-growth she stands ;
   And as she sways the branches with her hands,
Along her arm the sundered bloom falls sheer,
In separate petals shed, each like a tear ;
   While from the quivering bough the bird expands
   His wings. And lo ! thy spirit understands
Life shaken and shower'd and flown, and Death drawn
    near.

All stirs with change. Her garments beat the air :
   The angel circling round her aureole
   Shimmers in flight against the tree's gray bole :
While she, with reassuring eyes most fair,
A presage and a promise stands ; as 't were
   On Death's dark storm the rainbow of the Soul. .

THE DAY–DREAM.

(FOR A PICTURE.)

THE thronged boughs of the shadowy sycamore
   Still bear young leaflets half the summer through ;
   From when the robin 'gainst the unhidden blue
Perched dark, till now, deep in the leafy core,
The embowered throstle's urgent wood-notes soar
   Through summer silence.   Still the leaves come new ;
   Yet never rosy-sheathed as those which drew
Their spiral tongues from spring-buds heretofore.

Within the branching shade of Reverie
Dreams even may spring till autumn : yet none be
   Like woman's budding day-dream spirit-fann'd.
Lo ! tow'rd deep skies, not deeper than her look,
She dreams ; till now on her forgotten book
   Drops the forgotten blossom from her hand.

ASTARTE SYRIACA.

(FOR A PICTURE.)

Mystery : lo ! betwixt the sun and moon
 Astarte of the Syrians : Venus Queen
 Ere Aphrodite was. In silver sheen
Her twofold girdle clasps the infinite boon
Of bliss whereof the heaven and earth commune :
 And from her neck's inclining flower-stem lean
 Love-freighted lips and absolute eyes that wean
The pulse of hearts to the spheres' dominant tune.

Torch-bearing, her sweet ministers compel
 All thrones of light beyond the sky and sea
 The witnesses of Beauty's face to be :
That face, of Love's all-penetrative spell
Amulet, talisman, and oracle, —
 Betwixt the sun and moon a mystery.

PROSERPINA.

(PER UN QUADRO.)

Lungi è la luce che in sù questo muro
  Rifrange appena, un breve istante scorta
  Del rio palazzo alla soprana porta.
Lungi quei fiori d'Enna, O lido oscuro,
Dal frutto tuo fatal che omai m'è duro.
  Lungi quel cielo dal tartareo manto
  Che qui mi cuopre : e lungi ahi lungi ahi quanto
Le notti che saràn dai dì che furo.

Lungi da me mi sento ; e ognor sognando
  Cerco e ricerco, e resto ascoltatrice ;
  E qualche cuore a qualche anima dice,
(Di cui mi giunge il suon da quando in quando,
Continuamente insieme sospirando,) —
  " Oimè per te, Proserpina infelice ! "

PROSERPINA.

(FOR A PICTURE.)

AFAR away the light that brings cold cheer
   Unto this wall, — one instant and no more
   Admitted at my distant palace-door.
Afar the flowers of Enna from this drear
Dire fruit, which, tasted once, must thrall me here.
   Afar those skies from this Tartarean gray
   That chills me : and afar, how far away,
The nights that shall be from the days that were.

Afar from mine own self I seem, and wing
   Strange ways in thought, and listen for a sign :
   And still some heart unto some soul doth pine,
(Whose sounds mine inner sense is fain to bring,
Continually together murmuring,) —
   " Woe 's me for thee, unhappy Proserpine ! "

LA BELLA MANO.

(PER UN QUADRO.)

O BELLA Mano, che ti lavi e piaci
    In quel medesmo tuo puro elemento
    Donde la Dea dell' amoroso avvento
Nacque, (e dall' onda s'infuocar le faci
Di mille inispegnibili fornaci) : —
    Come a Venere a te l'oro e l'argento
    Offron gli Amori ; e ognun riguarda attento
La bocca che sorride e te che taci.

In dolce modo dove onor t' invii
    Vattene adorna, e porta insiem fra tante
    Di Venere e di vergine sembiante ;
Umilemente in luoghi onesti e pii
Bianca e soave ognora ; infin che sii,
    O Mano, mansueta in man d'amante.

LA BELLA MANO.

(FOR A PICTURE.)

O LOVELY hand, that thy sweet self dost lave
  In that thy pure and proper element,
  Whence erst the Lady of Love's high advènt
Was born, and endless fires sprang from the wave : —
Even as her Loves to her their offerings gave,
  For thee the jewelled gifts they bear ; while each
  Looks to those lips, of music-measured speech
The fount, and of more bliss than man may crave.

In royal wise ring-girt and bracelet-spann'd,
  A flower of Venus' own virginity,
Go shine among thy sisterly sweet band ;
  In maiden-minded converse delicately
  Evermore white and soft ; until thou be,
O hand ! heart-handsel'd in a lover's hand.

University Press : John Wilson & Son, Cambridge.

www.ingramcontent.com/pod-product-compliance
Lightning Source LLC
Chambersburg PA
CBHW020848020726
47497CB00005B/1302